"Are those homemade?"

Nate nodded to a plate of chocolate-chip cookies under a clear plastic dome beside the register of the Starfish Bay Mercantile.

Lindsey nodded. "Yes. This morning."

"Did you make them from your mother's recipe?"

Jolted, she stared at him.

The corners of his lips lifted again. "One of my happiest memories of this town is eating your mother's chocolate-chip cookies while we watched for whales from The Point."

Her mouth almost dropped open. She had sat with the junior version of this man eating cookies and watching for whales?

Again, she thought she detected a flash of disappointment in his eyes. But before she could be certain, he motioned toward the cookies. "I'll take two."

She filled his order and he quickly left. Lindsey watched until his car disappeared in the direction of the Orchid Motel.

Who *was* that guy?

And more importantly, why had he come back?

Books by Irene Hannon

Love Inspired

IRENE HANNON

writes both romance and romantic suspense and is an author of more than thirty-five novels, including the bestselling Heroes of Quantico series—*Against All Odds, An Eye For An Eye* and *In Harm's Way*. She is a two-time winner of the RITA® Award (the "Oscar®" of romantic fiction) and a five-time finalist. Her books have also been honored with a Daphne du Maurier award, two Reviewers' Choice awards from *RT Book Reviews* magazine and a Holt Medallion. A former corporate communications executive with a Fortune 500 company, Irene now writes full-time. She and her husband make their home in Missouri. For more information, Irene invites you to visit her website, www.irenehannon.com.

Seaside Reunion

Irene Hannon

Recycling programs
for this product may
not exist in your area.

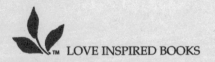 LOVE INSPIRED BOOKS

ISBN-13: 978-0-373-87715-7

SEASIDE REUNION

Copyright © 2012 by Irene Hannon

www.LoveInspiredBooks.com

Printed in U.S.A.

Dear Reader,

Welcome to Love Inspired!

2012 is a very special year for us. It marks the fifteenth anniversary of Love Inspired. Hard to believe that fifteen years ago, we first began publishing our warm and wonderful inspirational romances.

Back in 1997, we offered readers three books a month. Since then we've expanded quite a bit! In addition to the heartwarming contemporary romances of Love Inspired, we have the exciting romantic suspenses of Love Inspired Suspense, and the adventurous historical romances of Love Inspired Historical. Whatever your reading preference, we've got fourteen books a month for you to choose from now!

Throughout the year we'll be celebrating in several different ways. Look for books by bestselling authors who've been writing for us since the beginning, stories by brand-new authors you won't want to miss, special miniseries in all three lines, reissues of top authors and much, much more.

This is our way of thanking you for reading Love Inspired books. We know our uplifting stories of hope, faith and love touch your hearts as much as they touch ours.

Join us in celebrating fifteen amazing years of inspirational romance!

Blessings,

Melissa Endlich and Tina James
Senior Editors of Love Inspired Books

To Tom—
With wonderful memories of our Northern
California sojourn.

* * *

He will wipe every tear from their eyes,
and there shall be no more death or mourning,
wailing or pain, for the old order has passed away.
—*Revelation* 21:4

Chapter One

The bell over the front door of Starfish Bay Mercantile jingled, alerting Lindsey Collier to the arrival of a customer. Putting aside the town council meeting agenda she'd been perusing, she looked up with a smile. But her usual cheery greeting died in her throat.

The man who'd just stepped into the store was a stranger. A scruffy one.

And she didn't trust strangers.

Especially scruffy ones.

She gave the tall, lean, mid-thirtyish man a rapid scan. His dark brown hair needed a trim, his cobalt eyes were bloodshot, and his worn jeans and faded black T-shirt looked as if they'd been slept in—for several nights.

Standing slowly, she kept her eye on him as she edged toward the silent panic button—and the drawer that held her compact Beretta. "Can I help you?"

The man looked her way. For a long moment he studied her, faint furrows etching his brow. As if he were assessing her—or the security in the store.

Both were formidable—but she hoped she wouldn't have to prove that.

Swallowing past the fear congealing in her throat, she wrapped her fingers around the handle of the drawer and eased it open.

He cocked his head and squinted at her. "Lindsey Callahan?"

Her hand froze. She took another look at the stranger. Nothing about him was familiar, yet he knew her maiden name. "Have we met?"

The barest hint of a smile played at his lips. "A long time ago. Nate Garrison."

He didn't approach her, or extend his hand. That was good. She didn't want to be rude if she did happen to know this stranger, but neither did she intend to let her fingers stray far from the panic button—or the gun.

"I'm sorry...the name isn't ringing any bells."

He shoved his hands into the pockets of his jeans, a muted flash of disappointment echoing in the depths of his eyes. "You might remember me better as Nathaniel."

Nathaniel.

The image of a pale little boy with light brown hair and thick, always-smudged glasses flickered across her mind. But he'd come and gone quickly in her life, and she'd only been...what? Eight? Nine? She hadn't thought of him in years.

Her hand hovered over the gun. "You lived here once, right?"

"For a short time." He shifted around to survey the store. "This place hasn't changed much in twenty-five years."

"It hasn't changed much since 1936, when my grandfather opened it. We like it that way."

At her defensive tone, he swung back toward her. "I

wasn't being critical. It's nice to know some things stay the same."

"Very few." She withdrew her hand from her security cache. But she left the drawer open. "So are you passing through?"

"No." He moved closer, hands still in pockets. "I'll be around a while. I stopped here to pick up some food and see if I could get a recommendation for a place to stay."

She narrowed her eyes. "If you're looking for work, there isn't much to be had except at the fishing camps, and as far as I know, neither of them are hiring. Tourism in northern California has been down all season."

"I didn't come here for a job."

Then what did *you come for?*

The question hung between them, unasked and unanswered.

When the silence lengthened, she gave him another once-over. No pricey accommodations for this guy. "There's a low-key bed and breakfast a couple of streets over. Or the Orchid Motel, on the north end of town. I expect there are some houses and apartments available by the month, too. Depends on how long you're planning to stay."

"I have no idea. But I don't want to commit to a monthly rental. And I'm not a B&B kind of guy. Is the motel clean?"

"Eat-off-the-floor. Two older sisters from Georgia bought it about a dozen years ago, and they hate dirt. The attached café is excellent, too. They're both great cooks."

"Sold." He smiled, and as the angular lines of his face softened, an odd—and unwelcome—tingle zipped up her spine.

She broke eye contact on the pretext of checking her watch. "You might need a snack to tide you over. The café won't be open again until five. And for future reference, breakfast is seven to nine. Lunch, eleven to one. Dinner, five to seven. Closed on Sundays. Like clockwork."

"Thanks. I'll remember." He ambled over to the refrigerated case, inspected the display, and pulled out a can of soda and a prepackaged deli sandwich. On his way back to the counter, he snagged a cellophane-wrapped brownie—but he held it back as she rang up his purchases. "Are those homemade?" He nodded to a plate of chocolate chip cookies under a clear plastic dome beside the register.

"Yes. This morning."

"Did you make them?"

She shifted under his scrutiny. "Yes."

"From your mother's recipe?"

Jolted, she stared at him.

His lips lifted again, creating a fan of lines at the corners of his eyes. "One of my happiest memories of this town is eating your mother's chocolate chip cookies while we watched for whales from The Point."

Her mouth almost dropped open. She had sat with the junior version of this man eating cookies and watching for whales? A fuzzy, fleeting memory surfaced of a long-ago summer day at The Point. Ice cream had somehow been involved. But it was gone before she could catch hold of it.

Again, she thought she detected a flash of disappointment in his eyes. But before she could be certain, he motioned toward the cookies and riffled through his wallet. "I'll take two."

In silence, Lindsey rang them up and put them in a white deli bag. On impulse, she added a third one.

"Hey…that's too many. I only paid for two."

She crimped the top of the bag and handed it to him. "For old time's sake." Why she felt the need to make amends for forgetting him was beyond her. But the tiny glimmer of gratitude in his blue irises told her she'd done the right thing.

"Thanks." He picked up his purchases. "I'll see you around."

With that he exited, the bell announcing his departure just as it had marked his arrival.

Lindsey shifted her position behind the counter, stepping into the late-afternoon shadows so she could see without being seen. She expected him to climb into some old jalopy or mount a motorcycle, but the only car in the lot besides her six-year-old Camry was a newer model Acura.

Huh.

The man had some bucks after all.

She watched as he slid into the driver's seat, all six-foot-plus of him. Rather than start the engine, though, he dipped his head. His shoulders flexed. Then he lifted a chocolate chip cookie, took a big bite and closed his eyes as he chewed.

Was he relishing the taste—or the memories it stirred?

He ate the whole cookie that way, eyes closed, expression pensive. When he finished, he popped the top on the soda can, took a swig and started the engine.

Craning her neck, she watched until his car disappeared in the direction of the Orchid Motel.

Who *was* that guy?

And more important, why had he come back?

* * *

Nate had no trouble finding the Orchid Motel. It was right on Highway 101, just past the five-block-long main street. A gaudy purple orchid decorated the hand-painted sign above the door of the café.

As he pulled into the small parking lot, he eyed the low, white building with eight numbered doors to the right. The paint was fresh, the windows clean and a planter overflowing with flowers in all their August splendor stood beside each door. If the inside was as well maintained, it would do nicely.

And it was a lot better than some of the rat holes he'd bunked in during his stint in Afghanistan.

Stifling those memories, he set the brake, finished off his soda in three long gulps, and slid out of the car. A trip to The Point was high on his priority list, but better to secure a room and exorcise some of the road grunge first. The Point had waited twenty-five years for his return. It could wait another hour or two.

A Closed sign in the door of the café directed motel guests to ring the adjacent bell, and he followed the instructions. A muffled musical peal sounded in the recesses of the dim building.

As he waited for someone to answer the summons, he took a deep breath of the clean, salt-tanged air. It felt good to be home. Or the only place he'd ever thought of as home, despite his brief sojourn here. Finding the Mercantile largely unchanged had been a balm to his soul, even if he'd been disappointed Lindsey had forgotten him. But what had he expected? She might have been a central figure in the best few months of his childhood, but he'd been nothing more than a blip in *her* life.

The friendly little girl with the golden-haired ponytail and animated brown eyes had grown into a beautiful woman, though. Tall and slender, she'd retained the innate kindness that had drawn him as a child. Her cookie gesture told him that. But there were changes, too. Her hair, while still touched with gold, had darkened a few shades. And the enthusiasm that had once sparked in her eyes had been tempered. By life, no doubt.

He could relate.

A blur of motion on the other side of the door caught his attention, and he summoned up a smile as a white-haired woman fiddled with the lock. Based on Lindsey's skeptical perusal, his disheveled state wasn't making the best impression. But a nonstop cross-country drive could do that to a person. Until he had a chance to freshen up, all he could do to counter his off-putting appearance was be extra friendly. Even if that taxed his rusty social skills to the limit.

There hadn't been much time for niceties on the battlefield.

When the door was at last pulled open, the savory aroma of herbs and roasting meat wafted out, setting off a rumble in his stomach. The woman on the other side adjusted her glasses and gave him an apologetic eye roll. "Sorry for the delay, young man. You'd think I'd have mastered this lock by now. We had it installed six months ago. Come in, come in. Are you needing a room?"

Nate stepped past her. "Yes. If you have a vacancy."

"Plenty of space." She shut the door behind him and led the way to a stool-lined counter that doubled as the motel check-in desk. "Things have been slow this summer. The economy and all that. Not that we've ever been the most bustling place around." She grinned at him and pulled out a bulging registration book, with corners of envelopes, letters and brochures sticking out on three sides. "Mostly we get fishermen and redwood gawkers. Which camp do you fall into?"

"Neither."

She peered at him over the top of her glasses. "Not much else to do around here. You just passing through for the night?"

"No. I'll be here for a week, at least."

"Excellent. I can give you the weekly rate, then." She beamed at him and named a price that sounded more than fair. "So...are you visiting family or friends?" She dug a pen out of a drawer beside a decades-old cash register.

"Small towns are all alike. Everyone always wants to know your business."

His father's complaint, long dormant in Nate's memory, abruptly resurfaced. That had been a constant refrain in Chuck Garrison's litany of grievances—and one of his standard excuses whenever they'd moved. *Excuse* being the operative word. He'd never been able to face the real reason they'd had to lead a nomadic life.

But Nate had learned that not all questions were prompted by nosiness. Sometimes people's interest was sincere.

"No. I lived here for a few months many years ago. This place has good memories for me."

The woman handed him the pen, angled the registration book toward him and tapped an empty line. "Visits to the past don't always turn out quite the way we expect. I hope yours does."

"Thanks." He signed on the line and gave the ancient cash register a doubtful look. "Do you take credit cards?"

She perused his signature, then wrinkled her nose. "Yes. From motel guests only. We finally caved a few years back. Nobody carries cash these days, and too many checks bounced." She rummaged around under the counter and pulled out a manual credit-card machine. The kind that required carbon paper. He hadn't seen one in years.

After paying for the full week, Nate slid the credit card back into his wallet.

"Room six. That's my personal favorite. And we just put in a new TV." She smiled at him as she held out the key.

"Any chance you have internet connections in the rooms?" He took the orchid-bedecked ring.

Her smile dimmed. "No. Sorry." She gestured to the cash register. "As you can see, we're a bit behind the times. My sister has a computer in the office, and she's quite the whiz at it. But she hasn't convinced me to get one in here yet. If you need to go online, though, the Mercantile added a little coffee nook a while back, and I've seen people in there using their laptops."

Funny he hadn't noticed that.

Then again, he'd been a little distracted by his encounter with Lindsey.

"I'll check it out. Thanks."

The woman extended her hand, cheery smile once more in place. "By the way, I'm Genevieve Durham. If you need anything at all during your stay, you let me or my sister, Lillian, know. We live upstairs."

Nate took her hand, and she gripped his fingers with surprising firmness. "Thank you. And I'll be back for dinner. Whatever's cooking smells great."

"Tonight's special. Homemade pot roast. It's been

simmering all afternoon." Eyes twinkling, she gave him a wink. "If I do say so myself, I make the best pot roast in the county. Just be here by seven."

He smiled. "I'll be here at five."

Chuckling, she slid the registration book back under the counter. "Lillian baked blackberry pie for dessert, too. It goes quick."

"Save me a piece, okay?" He returned the wink.

Color spilled onto her cheeks. "I'll do that. And if no one's welcomed you back yet to Starfish Bay, let me be the first."

Lindsey had welcomed him back—sort of—with that extra cookie. After she'd gotten past her obvious suspicions. He didn't share that with this woman, though.

"Thanks." He started toward the door, but as he reached for the knob, she called after him.

"I hope you find whatever it is you're looking for, Mr. Garrison."

He turned toward her, impressed by her astuteness. "It's Nate. And I hope so, too."

But as he exited the café and returned to his car, he didn't have a lot of confidence that hope would be realized.

Because truth be told, he wasn't certain what had compelled him to make the marathon drive from Chicago to this tiny Pacific coast town. Nor did he know what he was seeking.

All he knew was that in the wee hours of a cold, high-desert morning in Afghanistan several weeks ago, with the distant echo of bombs sending tremors through the ground beneath his ear, this idea had popped into his head. An idea his gut had told him to pursue.

And he always listened to his gut.

* * *

"Do I smell chili, Dad?" Lindsey wiped her feet on the mat and shut the back door.

From his position in front of the stove, Jack Callahan hitched himself around to smile at her. "Bingo. I got in the mood to do some cooking today."

"Mmm." She joined him and took a whiff from the pot. "Did you put in plenty of jalapeños and chili powder?"

He chuckled as he stirred. "Where did you get that cast-iron stomach of yours, anyway?"

Grinning, she filched half a jalapeño from the cutting board on the counter and popped it into her mouth. "Mom liked hot stuff."

"True." He stirred the pot and gave her an impish look. "Guess that's why she went for me."

Lindsey wrinkled her nose and nudged him with her shoulder. Gently. It was bad enough the limp he'd acquired after breaking his hip two years ago had left him with some balance issues. She didn't want any more falls—or midnight calls from the ER. "Cute."

"Anything interesting happen at the store today?"

"As a matter of fact, yes." She opened the cutlery drawer and pulled out utensils. "I had a customer who said he'd lived here years ago. I have sort of a vague recollection of a little boy with his name, but your memory is probably better than mine. Nathaniel Garrison."

Her father's eyebrows rose as he dished up the chili. "Now there's a name from the past. He and his parents lived here twenty, twenty-five years ago for a few months. His father worked in a warehouse in Crescent City, I think. They kept to themselves, though we did see the boy and his mother at church on Sundays. That's how the two of you met. You were quite a pair for a few months. Spent hours watching for whales at The Point, as I recall."

"He mentioned that." Lindsay furrowed her brow. "I wonder why my memory about that is so hazy."

"Now that I think about it, you couldn't have been more than eight or nine at the time. Most people don't remember much from that age." He ladled one more scoop of chili into the second bowl. "Nathaniel was a nice little boy. On the quiet side."

"He goes by Nate now."

"Does he?" Her father deposited their bowls on the table while she filled glasses with water. "What's he doing here?"

"He didn't say." She set the glasses on the table and took her seat. "So why did his family live here for such a short time?"

Her father retrieved a basket of cornbread from the counter, then lowered himself into his chair. "There was some sort of scandal, best I can recall. Had to do with his father drinking and getting fired, if my memory serves me correctly. They left not long after that."

"That's strange." Lindsey draped her napkin over her lap. "You'd think that would be a bad memory for a little boy. But he said he had happy memories of his time here. He even mentioned Mom's chocolate chip cookies."

"Well, they *were* memorable." Her father helped himself to a piece of bread and tucked it on the plate beside his bowl of chili. "You want to say the blessing tonight?

"Why don't you do it?" He asked the same question every night; she always gave the same response. Even after three years, prayer was hard for her.

As if reading her mind, her father's expression softened and he gentled his voice. "You ever going to make your peace with the Lord, Lindy?"

Her throat contracted at his pet name for her. "I'm trying, Dad."

He sighed and patted her hand. "I know, honey. And you keep at it. One of these days, you'll get the answers you need."

"God's been silent for a long time."

"But He's been listening. Don't forget that." With one more pat of her hand, her father bowed his head and started the blessing.

Lindsey didn't pay a lot of attention to her father's prayer. Her mind kept drifting to the odd encounter this afternoon. But her ears perked up when he got to the end.

"And Lord, we ask you to help Nathaniel find whatever it is he's looking for here in Starfish Bay. Amen." He reached for his spoon and dug into his chili.

Curious, Lindsey picked up her own spoon. "That was an interesting request. What makes you think he's looking for something here?"

"Do you think he came to fish or sightsee?"

She frowned, spoon poised over her bowl. "No. He doesn't have the look of a sportsman or tourist. But why else would he come here?"

"He didn't just come. He came *back*. There's a difference."

Yeah, there was. She knew that firsthand.

She also knew people went back to places for a lot of reasons. Some good, some bad.

And if Nate Garrison was lucky, his reasons—unlike hers—were good.

Chapter Two

Three hours after checking in at the Orchid, fortified with the best meal he'd had in years and rejuvenated by a hot shower and unplanned nap, Nate exited his room and locked the door.

It was time to visit The Point.

He crossed the gravel parking lot that separated the motel from the two-lane highway, debating his route to the headland—the hidden cut-through path from town he and Lindsey had always used, or the gravel access road to the north, just around the bend?

The road was closer—and would be easier to find after all these years. He struck out to the north.

As he rounded the bend less than five minutes later, Nate frowned. In the old days, the road had always been open and welcoming. Now, a rusty chain barred access, and a Private Property sign further discouraged visitors.

Stopping in front of the chain, he propped his fists on his hips. It had never occurred to him the property would be off-limits. Perhaps the small white chapel where he'd attended Sunday services wasn't even there anymore. And what about the stone bench with the sweeping vista of the sea, where he'd first spoken with Lindsey?

After a brief hesitation, Nate skirted the barrier and set off down the rutted road. You didn't get to be an ace combat reporter by letting intimidation tactics deter you. If he did meet anyone who accused him of trespassing, he'd tell them he'd traveled thousands of miles just to see this spot from his childhood. Most people were suckers for stories like that, as he'd learned while honing his reporting skills. A tug on the heartstrings was far more effective than quoting the number of troops killed in a battle. It was always better to put a face on the statistic. Focus on one soldier's story.

But he hoped he wouldn't have to resort to dramatics. He preferred to make this journey into the past alone. If he was lucky, the place would be deserted.

As he traversed the forest-rimmed lane, it was clear no vehicles had driven on the pothole-pitted surface in a long time. The only sign of life was a blacktail deer that shot him a wary glance from the shadowy woods as he passed.

He didn't slow his pace until he rounded a bend and the barren tip of the headland came into sight, soaring high above the Pacific. Then he stopped, drinking in the view that swept him back twenty-five years.

In the far distance, a slight haze softened the line where sea and sky met. To his right and left, other headlands jutted into the blue water along the irregular coast, their steeply sloping rock faces supporting forested or barren tops, some of them wrapped in horizontal tendrils of cloud. Offshore from the tiny beaches and cliff bases, jagged boulders thrust through the surface of the water, aiming for the sky as the surf churned around them.

From his position, Nate couldn't see the rocks below The Point. But the muted thunder of crashing waves and the periodic geysers of mist rising above the top of the headland told him they were still there.

Nothing in the natural setting had changed.

But the same couldn't be said of the chapel across the rutted gravel parking lot.

The small clapboard structure, with its steep roof and spire, had once been white. Now it sported weathered gray patches where the paint had peeled away. The windows were boarded up, the front door secured with a rusty padlock, and the manicured lawn and garden that had once surrounded the structure had become a tangle of tall grasses and weeds. Only a few hardy flowers had managed to poke their heads above the mess.

This wasn't what he'd expected.

Disappointment welled up inside him. Not just over the sad state of the chapel, but also for what the disrepair meant.

Reverend Tobias—the man who'd given him hope when his world had turned black—must be gone.

Nate let out a long breath. It figured. Nothing stayed the same.

Especially good things.

Quashing his sense of letdown, Nate wandered across the gravel lot and inspected the weed-covered stepping-stone path that led to the front door. Although the padlock told him he wouldn't be able to get inside, he plowed through the tangled undergrowth, brushing aside the tall grass in his path. One of the three steps that led to the small porch was missing, as was one side of the railing, and the porch planks creaked ominously as his weight settled on them.

He moved toward one of the small side windows beside the door. Maybe there was a crack in the boards that would afford him a glimpse of the interior.

But a quick scan dashed that hope. The place was sealed up tight.

Resigned, he retraced his route to the parking lot. There wasn't much chance the bench behind the chapel that he and Lindsey had once sat on would still be there, but as long as he was here it was worth a look.

Thirty seconds later, rounding the church, he again halted.

The bench was there. In pristine condition, surrounded by a tiny square of tended lawn and flanked by two pots overflowing with flowers.

And it was occupied.

Lindsey sat facing away from him, a watering can at her feet, her attention fixed on the horizon as the rays of the setting sun highlighted the gold in her hair and silhouetted her slender, jeans-clad form.

The corners of Nate's mouth lifted. The only thing missing from the picture was a sack of chocolate chip cookies, a pair of binoculars and the innocence of childhood.

His smile faded.

Maybe Thomas Wolfe was right.

Maybe you couldn't go home again.

He started to turn away, but in his peripheral vision he saw Lindsey jump to her feet and spin toward him. He angled back.

She stared at him, posture taut, expression uncertain. "Nate?"

One side of his mouth hitched up. "Yeah. I clean up pretty well, don't I?"

Instead of answering his question, she asked one of her own. "What are you doing here?"

"Trespassing, it seems. Though reminiscing had been my intent." He gestured toward the chapel. "What happened?"

She tucked her fingers into the front pockets of her jeans, the stiffness in her shoulders easing. "Reverend Tobias died three years ago. We couldn't find a replacement, so people started attending churches in other towns." She surveyed the decaying structure, the muscles working in her throat as she swallowed. "Starfish Bay owns this headland, and the original plan was to turn it into a park and rent out the chapel for special-occasion use. But there's never been money available for restoration, and the chapel isn't old enough to qualify as an official historic landmark. We can't even afford to keep up the maintenance."

"That small spot is in great condition." He nodded toward the area where she stood.

She picked up the watering can, keeping the bench between them. "I still like to come out here. So I reclaimed this from the weeds." She edged toward the end of the bench, as if she wanted to escape.

But he didn't want her to go. Being here with her again felt good. And right.

"So you never left Starfish Bay?"

A cloud passed over the setting sun, casting a shadow in her eyes. Or was there another reason for the sudden darkening of her irises?

"I moved away for a few years."

She offered nothing more, but he knew how to put people at ease. Loosen their tongues. It was part of his job, even if he hadn't used those skills much recently.

Digging deep, he smiled, shoved his hands into his

pockets and adopted a casual, relaxed stance. "Anywhere interesting?"

"Sacramento."

"What took you there?"

Her grip on the watering can tightened, and she hugged it closer to her body. "That's where my husband lived."

Lived.

Past tense.

Nate processed that new information as his gaze dropped to the ringless third finger of her left hand. She must be divorced. "So what brought you back here?"

"He died."

That wasn't the response he'd expected.

"I'm sorry." Even as the trite words left his mouth, he berated himself. Talk about lame. Words were his business. He should have been able to come up with a more empathetic response than that.

"Thanks." She started to ease around the bench again.

He wanted her to leave even less now that she'd dropped her bombshell. Yet asking questions was driving her away. Time to switch tactics, try to pique her interest with a few personal revelations.

"I can't imagine losing a spouse. I guess that's one of the reasons I'm still single. Besides, my job isn't conducive to marriage."

She stopped and gave him a curious look. "What do you do?"

"I'm a journalist. Investigative for a while. But for the past year I've been doing combat coverage in Afghanistan for the *Chicago Tribune*."

Her eyes widened. "Were you embedded with a unit?"

"Yes."

"Wow. That's risky work."

He lifted one shoulder. "The soldiers did the really dangerous stuff."

She squinted at him. "Not from what I've seen on the news. Some of those reporters seem to be in the thick of things."

"Writing for a newspaper is different than TV coverage." And often worse. But he didn't share that.

She set the watering can on the seat of the bench. A positive sign.

"So what brought you here? This is a long way from Chicago or Afghanistan."

His fingers tightened into fists inside his pockets as he struggled to maintain a placid demeanor even as the sounds of an explosion echoed in his mind. "I needed a change of scene, so I took a six-week leave and decided to do some traveling here in the U.S." He motioned to the bench. "Do you mind if we sit? I've been driving for thirty-three hours and the nap I took at the motel wasn't nearly long enough."

She hesitated, then perched on the far end of the bench—as if poised to flee. She left the watering can between them.

Following her lead, he sat on the other end, as close to the edge as possible. Funny. As kids, he'd been the cautious, reserved one while Lindsey had been the gregarious risk taker. Now their roles seemed reversed. Why?

Whatever the reason, he suspected she wasn't going to reveal it today.

"Is the room okay?"

Her question refocused him. "Fine. Spotless, as promised." He shifted around to look at the chapel, now cast in warm light from the setting sun. "Too bad about this place. It has some good memories for me."

"Me, too." She tipped her head and caught her lower lip between her teeth as she eyed him, a habit he suddenly recalled from their childhood. She'd always done that at her most serious moments. Or if she had something on her mind.

He gave her an encouraging smile. "I don't recall you ever being shy about expressing your thoughts when we were kids. If you have a question, go ahead and ask." Perhaps if he gave her carte blanche, she'd reciprocate.

"I mentioned you to my dad at dinner." Her tone was cautious. Tentative. "From what he remembered, it didn't sound as if your family situation was the kind that would give you a lot of happy memories of this place. Or make you want to return."

Once again, she'd blindsided him. He hadn't expected her to touch on such a personal subject.

Nate stood, shoved his hands into his pockets, and took a couple of steps toward the edge of the cliff as he debated how to respond. From here, he could see the waves crashing on the rocks below, where the frolicking seals had often entertained them. Farther down was the stretch of deserted sand that had hosted their beachcombing excursions on several occasions. Lifting his head, he scanned the far horizon, where passing ships had inspired them to make up stories about adventures and travels that would take them far beyond Starfish Bay.

How could he tell this wary woman *she* was one of the reasons he had happy memories of his brief sojourn in this tiny town?

He couldn't. Not without spooking her. But sharing the other reason his time here had been idyllic presented another problem.

He didn't talk about his painful past. Ever. With anyone.

Then again, Lindsey wasn't just anyone. She was the best friend he'd ever had.

Could he make an exception for her?

From her seat on the bench, Lindsey studied the broad back and strong profile of the man standing a few feet off to the side. There was little about him to remind her of the shy, timid boy who'd been forever pushing his glasses up his nose and who, she suddenly recalled, had greeted all of her adventurous plans with trepidation.

A memory flitted through her mind, of a hike they'd taken down to the beach once to look for agates. She'd had to push and prod him all the way, though once there he'd entered into the search with gusto. How odd, to think a boy like that would end up choosing a career that took him to trouble spots and put him in the line of fire.

Just as Mark had.

A familiar pang of sorrow engulfed her, but before it became suffocating, Nate spoke.

"How much did your dad know about my family situation?"

Pulling herself back from the past, she chose her words with care. "Very little. And all based on hearsay. The story was that you moved not long after your dad lost his job in Crescent City. There was talk he'd been drinking."

Nate snorted. "It was more than talk. Dad was an alcoholic who couldn't hold a job for more than a few months, at best. Every time he got fired, we moved. That's why my mom homeschooled me."

He stopped, and Lindsey wondered if that was all he was going to offer. But then he picked up the story.

"One day, she'd had enough. She threatened to leave him if he didn't get his act together. He promised he would, and she agreed to give him one more chance. That's when we moved here. And for nine months, from April until December, he kept his promise. We were a real family. We ate dinner together. Went on outings. Dad even attended church with us once in a while. It was the best time of my life. Until he started drinking again and everything fell apart." His voice rasped.

In the hush that followed, broken only by the crash of the waves below and the caw of the gulls above, Lindsey mulled over what he'd said. And spotted the gap at once. He'd told her *why* he'd come back. But he hadn't told her why he'd come back *now*.

That wasn't a question she felt comfortable asking, however. The sudden shakiness in his words and the taut line of his shoulders told her she'd pushed far enough into personal territory for one day. Territory she suspected he usually traveled solo. In light of that, she was surprised—and touched—he'd told her as much as he had.

"I can see why this place is special to you." Warmth crept into her voice. "And Starfish Bay does have a way of calling people back."

"Yeah." He kept his face averted. Cleared his throat. "Besides, I was overdue for a vacation. And I needed to get away for a while."

Why?

Again the question hovered on the tip of her tongue. Again, she bit it back. And moved to safer ground. "Everyone needs time off and a change of scene once in a while. I used to look forward to the summer vacation when I taught."

"You're a teacher?" He turned toward her.

"Was. I just tutor a little now and run the Mercantile with my dad."

"When did you come back from Sacramento?"

"Three years ago."

"After your husband died?"

"Yes." Lindsey grabbed the handle of the watering can and stood. That subject wasn't open for discussion. "Dad fell and broke his hip, and he needed help with the store. So I moved back."

"I thought your mom worked at the store, too."

Another pang of sorrow echoed in her heart. "She died when I was twelve."

Nate's expression softened. "I'm sorry to hear that. She was a nice woman."

"Yeah. She was." Lindsey shifted the can to her other hand. "Look, I need to get back."

"And miss the sunset?" He gestured to the sky.

It *was* glorious. Above, the sky was still deep blue. But closer to the water, bands of pink, yellow and orange streaked across the horizon, casting a rose-colored glimmer on the water. Normally, she'd hang around for nature's finale. But for some odd reason, the idea of watching a sunset with this man felt dangerous. And her instincts told her the Beretta tucked into the concealed holster on her belt wouldn't protect her from the kind of threat he represented.

"Not tonight."

"May I walk you back to town?"

She took a step back, fighting down a flutter

of panic. "I'm fine. I do this all the time by myself. Thanks, anyway."

Without waiting for a response, she turned away and struck off toward the secret path that led to the center of town. The one she'd shown the child-size version of this man twenty-five years ago. Back when he'd been afraid of these woods.

As she reached the trees, she glanced over her shoulder. Nate had shifted over a few feet to keep her in sight. He lifted a hand in farewell. She responded, hoping he was too far away to see the disconcerting flush that crept over her cheeks.

And as she plunged into the woods, the route as familiar as her mom's cookie recipe, she had a feeling the grown-up Nathaniel wasn't afraid of the woods anymore.

Or very much else.

Nate watched Lindsey until the shadows in the woods swallowed her. Then he retook his seat on the bench, his thoughts on their encounter rather than the last act of the sunset playing out before him.

He hadn't planned to spill his guts about his family to anyone in Starfish Bay. But Lindsey's caring demeanor had invited confidences, just as it had in the old days. No surprise there.

His own reaction, however, had startled him. He'd thought he'd long ago stowed the emotional baggage from his childhood.

But this place was dragging it out again.

A silhouetted ship on the horizon caught his attention, the vessel a mere speck in the vast expanse of water. Moving steadily toward a specific destination, it would continue to plow through the sea, undeterred by squalls or darkness, floundering only if its navigation and communications system went down. Then, it could lose its way.

Kind of like he had.

As he faced that hard, cold fact, he took a deep breath and wrapped his fingers around the solid edge of the stone bench that had withstood more than its share of storms. The truth was, he felt adrift. And had for a long time. But his unsettled feeling had been more intense since the bombing.

Maybe that's why he'd made his marathon cross-country drive to Starfish Bay. Perhaps deep inside he'd harbored a hope that this place could show him how to recapture the joy he'd known here.

But now that he was back, where would he find the guidance he needed?

A rattle sounded behind him, and he shifted on the bench to look over his shoulder. The wind had picked up, and as a flapping shingle on the roof of the chapel drew his eye, the clouds on the horizons parted. All at once a ray of sun peeked through, bathing the steeple in a golden glow.

Almost like a sign.

Nate's lips twisted into a humorless smile. Now that was a stretch. Next thing, he'd be thinking it was God who had urged him, on that desert night in Afghanistan, to make this journey.

As if God cared.

"God does care, Nathaniel. And He always answers our prayers. Sometimes not in the way we expect, but that's because He knows better than we do what's best for us. There's a purpose in everything. Trust Him."

Reverend Tobias's long-forgotten words suddenly echoed in Nate's mind. The kindly man had spoken them on this very bench, when he'd found Nate huddled here, crying, the night before his family had moved again. And Nate had clung to them for months, doing his best to believe, trusting that the man had spoken the truth and God would show him why He'd turned his life upside down.

That had never happened. Then tragedy had struck again. So he'd looked elsewhere for meaning.

And come up just as empty.

Now here he was, back in the place where an idyllic time and a devout man had fueled his passion for God.

Coincidence? Maybe not.

Because truth be told, he had a feeling only God could answer the question that had plagued him since he'd lay among those dead and dying soldiers.

Why me?

Chapter Three

❧

This can't be happening!

The words echoed in Lindsey's mind as she stared at the man in the dark business suit, crisp white shirt and silk tie who was placing a glossy, mounted photo on an easel in the town hall.

"That's correct, Mayor Peroni. It would be a very upscale, exclusive resort, much like this one that we built on the Kona Coast in Hawaii." He positioned the easel so it could be seen by the four town council members and the mayor, who sat at a long table in the front of the hall, and by the three residents who'd wandered in to observe the monthly meeting. "Our guests prefer these types of secluded destinations. Near scenic areas, but off the beaten track. Your property certainly qualifies."

The man smiled.

Lindsey wanted to throw up.

A big-time developer wanted to buy The Point.

How had she missed that on the agenda?

She scanned the paper in front of her and reread the discussion items as the man launched into a spiel straight out of Sales 101. There it was. *Presentation on development project*. No wonder she'd read right over it. Talk about ambiguous. Leaning forward, she shot a dirty look at Dennis Simms, who handled the meeting minutes and the agenda. But he was engrossed in the man's slick presentation and the glossy photograph.

Lindsey sat back and gave the photo a closer inspection, too. Okay. The three-story structure was attractive. And yes, it was tasteful and blended well with the natural setting.

But no matter how well it was designed, any structure would still dominate the landscape and forever change The Point and the quaint ambience of Starfish Bay.

They couldn't let that happen.

"Excuse me." Lindsey raised her voice to interrupt the developer, who was gushing about the economic opportunities such a resort would offer the town, dangling terms like infusion of capital, job creation and enhanced infrastructure. Every eye in the place turned to her as the man stopped talking midsentence. "How much of The Point are you interested in buying?"

"All of it. The forested area between the resort and the town will act as a buffer zone for our guests."

"A buffer from what?"

A snicker came from the peanut gallery, and a flush rose on the man's neck. "Our guests prefer privacy when on resort property. But of course, many of them will also visit the town."

"To mingle with the riffraff? How nice." The man's color deepened, but Lindsey didn't give him a chance to respond. "What about the chapel on the property?"

He adjusted his tie. "According to our structural engineer, it's in poor condition. And we understand it's no longer in use. We're still working on preliminary architectural drawings, but I'm certain we would tear it down."

"I was baptized in that chapel."

Yes! Lindsey was tempted to give sixty-something Frank Martinez a thumbs-up for his comment. At least one council member was on her side.

"That doesn't make it a national shrine, Frank." Susan Peroni shot him an annoyed glance over her half glasses.

He glared back. "What about our plan to turn The Point into a park?"

"We don't have the money. You know that. We all know that. Parks are nice, but we're struggling to pay for the necessities. A resort like this could be a boon for the town."

Lindsey frowned at Susan as the developer's reference to a structural engineer suddenly registered. "You knew this was in the works, didn't you?"

The mayor shuffled the papers in front of her. "Louis Mattson himself called me a couple of days after the last council meeting. A very nice gentleman. Mattson Properties is a prestigious company known for its first-class resort projects, and he assured me the one on The Point would follow in those footsteps. I gave him permission to look the land over and do a preliminary site survey. In this economy, it's our civic duty to give an unbiased hearing to any opportunity that could bring new business to Starfish Bay."

Lindsey clamped her lips together and scowled at the mayor. Since Susan and her husband ran a local sightseeing company, they'd be among the biggest beneficiaries of an influx of tourists.

But so would other area businesses. She checked out the remaining two council members. Dennis ran a fishing camp, Janice operated an art gallery. More tourists would be beneficial for both of them.

Her stomach knotted.

The odds weren't looking good.

"I don't disagree with you, Susan." Janice folded her hands, twin furrows etching her brow. "In these economic times, we do need to consider all sources of revenue to bolster our town budget. But I'm not certain I like this idea. A resort like that," she gestured to the easel, "is lovely, but think how it would change the dynamics of the town. And as for The Point, I like the wild beauty of it, even if we never have the funds to make it a park. It's a tough decision."

So Janice wasn't gung ho on the idea, either. Maybe there was hope yet.

A hand rose at the back of the hall. Clint Nolan worked for the National Park Service and had degrees in marine biology and forestry. He'd only been in Starfish Bay for a year, but he was well respected. And he didn't like messing with nature or taming wild places. He might be an ally, too.

"Yes, Clint?" Susan tapped her pen against the table, the staccato rhythm echoing in the mostly empty hall.

He rose. "With due respect to the reputation of Mattson Properties, I have to agree with Janice. This sort of decision requires careful consideration and a full hearing before area residents. I'd suggest you schedule a meeting where we can see a more detailed plan for the site and listen to what other citizens have to say."

"Hear, hear." That from one of the other residents who'd attended the meeting.

"Well." Susan huffed and adjusted her glasses. "And here I thought this was a no-brainer. I had no idea a proposal with such obvious economic benefits to the community would be contentious."

The representative from the developer took down the photograph and folded up the easel. "I know Mr. Mattson would be happy to come himself and present some site renderings for residents to review. And to answer questions, of course."

"Does anyone on the council object to a special meeting?" When no one spoke, Susan sighed. "Okay. Let's talk dates."

Ten minutes later, after offering the developer a couple of options two weeks down the road, the meeting wrapped up.

As Lindsey gathered up her notes, Frank wandered over, obviously sensing a kindred spirit. "I'd hate to see that developer tear down the chapel and ruin The Point."

"Me, too."

"You think the town will go for it?"

"I hope not."

"He's a smooth talker, though." The man ran his fingers through his bristly white hair. "Think I might bend the Lord's ear a little on this one. See you around." With a wave, he walked toward the exit.

Lindsey followed close on his heels, hoping his prayer would be heard. Through all the turmoil and changes that had come her way, the headland and the chapel had been a stable, enduring element in her life. She'd found solace there in times of sorrow, joy in times of celebration, refuge in times of fear.

Losing it would be like losing part of herself.

Again.

So as she drove home through the night, she sent a simple but fervent plea of her own heavenward.

Please, Lord, help us preserve this special place.

* * *

Nate pushed through the front door of the Mercantile, the bell jingling overhead.

"I'll take care of it, honey." A masculine voice came from somewhere in the back of the store.

Spying a dome-covered plate of cookies near the cash register, Nate wandered over. Not chocolate chip today. But they looked tasty—even if he'd downed a hearty breakfast at the Orchid Café less than an hour and a half ago.

A movement to his right in the far corner of the store caught his eye, and he turned. A blond-haired boy, who appeared to be about ten or eleven, sat angled slightly toward him, elbow propped on the table, chin in hand, ankles wrapped around the legs of his chair. His expression was glum.

"You'll get it, Jarrod. I'll work with you until you do." Lindsey's encouraging words were muted.

Nate eased back for a better view. She was leaning across the small table toward the boy, posture intent.

"How can I help you?"

At the question, Nate swiveled away from the tableau in the opposite corner of the store toward the gray-haired man who was limping toward him. Nate didn't have a clear memory of Lindsey's father, but he could see the resemblance in the strong chin and shape of the mouth.

"Mr. Callahan?"

"None other." The older gent moved behind the counter. "Let me guess. Nathaniel Garrison. Or Nate now, so Lindsey tells me."

"None other."

The man chuckled and extended his hand, showing none of the wariness his daughter had exhibited on

Nate's first visit. "Welcome back to Starfish Bay. And it's Jack. Being addressed as mister by another adult makes me feel old."

Smiling, he returned Jack's firm grip. "Thank you. It's nice to be back."

"Hey, Lindsey, look who's here!"

At Jack's announcement, Nate shifted toward the duo again. Lindsey turned and leaned sideways. The light spilling in from the large front window drew attention to faint, half-moon shadows beneath her eyes and a pair of vertical creases above her nose that hadn't been there two days ago. He lifted his hand. Lindsey responded, then settled back into her chair, out of sight.

Not the warmest greeting he'd ever received.

"The sisters treating you okay at the Orchid?"

He refocused on Jack. "Like a son."

Jack grinned and propped a hip on the stool behind the counter. "That I can believe. They like to take care of people. When I broke my hip, they were at the house twice a day, like clockwork, delivering meals until Lindsey finished up the school year and could close things down in Sacramento. Have they baked you their famous cinnamon rolls yet?"

"No." His mouth started to water.

"They will if you stay long enough. That'll be a sure sign you've been adopted. Now what can I do for you today?"

"When I asked at the Orchid about internet connections, Genevieve pointed me here." He lifted his laptop case. "And I wouldn't mind trying a couple of those cookies. With some coffee." He gestured toward the dome.

"We do have Wi-Fi. Lindsey's idea. Make yourself at home over in the coffee nook. Also her idea." He gestured toward the far corner of the store as he eased back to his feet, grasping the edge of the counter for a moment to steady himself. "And the cookies are great. Ginger today. You'll like them."

Nate rested an elbow on the high, antique counter. "So what's going on back there?" He nodded to the coffee nook.

"A tutoring session. Jarrod's been having some problems at school, and Lindsey offered to try and help get him up to speed before the fall session starts next month. He comes three days a week." Jack deposited the cookies in a white sack and did a one-eighty toward the large urn on the back counter. "She was a teacher, you know."

"Yes. She told me."

Jack looked over his shoulder. "Is that right? You two must have had quite the conversation when you showed up Monday."

"She told me later that night. I took a walk out to The Point and ran into her."

"Room for cream?" Jack paused, hand on the dispensing lever.

"No. I take it black."

"I kind of figured that." He filled it to the brim, snapped on a plastic lid and set it on the counter. "Funny. Lindsey never mentioned she'd met up with you again."

Nate lifted one shoulder, unable to decipher the man's expression. But it made him a little uneasy. "It was impromptu. And brief. Sad thing about the chapel."

"Now that's a fact." The man sighed as he settled back on the stool, rang up Nate's purchases and took his money. "And it might get even sadder."

"What do you mean?"

As Lindsey's father told him about the developer's presentation at the town council meeting the prior night, Nate pocketed his change. "You think it will go through?"

Jack shrugged. "There's going to be another meeting in two weeks to give the residents a chance to voice their opinions and listen to the head honcho himself. But things are tough around here. And a resort like that would bring in a lot of new business. It'll come down to sentiment versus practicality, I'm thinking. Hard to say which way it will go. I wouldn't mind some extra business myself, but I'd hate to lose The Point. And Lindsey's beside herself. I heard her prowling around the house at all hours. I think she was up half the night."

That would explain the shadows under her eyes and the creases on her brow.

"I take it she was at the meeting?"

"Had to be. She's on the council."

As Nate digested that latest piece of news, the jangle of the bell over the door announced the arrival of another customer. He tucked his laptop case under his arm and picked up his coffee and cookies. "Time to go to work."

"I thought you were here on vacation."

"Can't escape email." Flashing the man a smile, he headed toward the coffee nook.

And nook was the right word. Three small tables for two were tucked into the far corner beside a large picture window that offered a distant glimpse of the sea on the opposite side of the highway.

Lindsey and the boy looked up as he approached. He lifted his cup and indicated the computer under his arm. "I hear this is the spot for Wi-Fi."

She motioned toward the two empty tables. "Help yourself."

Nate set the cup and cookies on the one closest to the window, took a seat and pulled out his laptop. As he waited for it to boot up, he sipped the coffee and listened to the conversation a few feet away.

"Let's try another one, Jarrod. Remember, even problems that sound complicated can be simple if you break them down into small pieces." She positioned a piece of paper on the table so they could both see it as she read. "'Jason and Mark went to lunch at a café. They ordered a chicken wrap for $6.50, a hamburger and French fries for $7.95, and two glasses of lemonade for $1.25 each. The tax was $1.35. They gave the waiter $20.00. How much change should they receive?' Okay. Let's start by adding up the wrap and the burger."

Lindsey patiently walked Jarrod through the problem step by step, offering encouragement when he made mistakes and praise for correct answers. Impressive. She must have been some teacher.

As Nate opened the white sack and took out a cookie, Jack walked over to Lindsey. "Frank Martinez is on the line. You want to talk to him or call him back?"

"I'll talk to him. It's about last night's meeting." She rose and put another sheet of paper in front of Jarrod. "Work on this while I'm gone, okay? Break it down, like we did with the last one. I'll be right back."

His laptop now booted, Nate clicked on the email icon and entered his password. Fifty-one messages came up.

So much for getting away from it all.

As he set his cookie down, he glanced over at Jarrod and caught the boy watching him. The youngster's cheeks reddened and he dipped his head over the paper, his glasses slipping down his nose. The same way Nate's had done as a kid.

And there was another similarity, too.

The boy's eyes held a deep, abiding sadness.

Most people probably wouldn't notice it. They'd just see a quiet kid who kept to himself and didn't laugh a whole lot. But problems in school didn't make a boy look that sad. There was something deeper going on with the youngster seated a few feet away.

Nate had been there.

And it was a tough place.

The boy peeked at him again, and Nate smiled. "Hi."

His flush rose higher, but he mumbled a response. "Hi."

"You like cookies?"

A spark of interest flared in the boy's eyes. "Yeah."

"Want my other one? I'm full." Nate held up the bag.

Jarrod regarded it. "I'm not supposed to take presents from strangers."

"A cookie doesn't qualify as a present. And I'm not really a stranger. I'm Lindsey's friend."

The boy squinted. "What does *qualify* mean?"

"It means it doesn't count. Now a bike or an iPod or a trip to Disney World—that would qualify as a present."

Jarrod started to reach for the bag, but jerked his hand back as Lindsey approached.

"What's going on?" She stopped beside the table.

"I have an extra cookie." Nate gave the bag a little shake. "I thought your student might like it."

"Mom told me not to take presents from strangers. But he," the boy pointed at him, "said he's your friend. Is he?"

Lindsey darted a quick look at him, a faint flush tinting her cheeks. "I knew him when I was a little girl. It's okay if you take the cookie. And I just saw your mom pull up."

She hadn't confirmed they were friends.

Nate tamped down his flicker of disappointment.

Eyeing the cookie bag, the youngster approached him.

"My name is Nate." He handed it over. "You're Jarrod, right?"

The boy nodded as he took the bag, crimping the top tight in his fingers.

"Enjoy that cookie, okay?"

"Okay."

Lindsey finished collecting the papers and started toward the front door. "Let's go meet your mom."

The boy trailed after her, stopping as he reached a shelving unit that would hide him from Nate's view once he passed. "Thank you."

Nate smiled at him. "You're welcome. Maybe I'll see you around again sometime."

He didn't get an answering smile. Or a response. But that was okay. Kids like that just needed to know someone had noticed them. And cared. He might not be able to fix whatever problems plagued Jarrod's young life, but he could at least offer that much.

Before he left the Mercantile today, though, he'd see what he could find out about the boy's background.

And hope Lindsey would share more of Jarrod's story than she'd been willing to share of her own.

Chapter Four

"Is this stuff any good, Lindsey?" Janice wandered over to the check-out counter with a bottle of an all-natural beverage.

"You want the truth, one town council member to another?"

Janice grinned. "Yeah."

"To me, it tastes like medicine. But a lot of the cyclists who stop in ask for it, so we started to stock it."

"Thanks for the heads-up. Think I'll pass. Give me two of those ginger cookies instead."

"Smart choice."

At Nate's comment, Lindsey looked toward the coffee nook to find him strolling toward them. Too bad her father had gone home for lunch and a nap. Otherwise, she'd have found some excuse to leave the Mercantile in his hands for a couple of hours. Because for whatever reason, Nate made her nervous.

"Take the word of someone who's already sampled one and intends to buy another." He joined them at the counter as he finished his endorsement.

Lindsey's pulse gave a sudden blip as the scent of

his subtle aftershave wafted toward her. How weird was that?

"Sold. Ring me up two, Lindsey."

"And one more for me," Nate added.

She left them to their small talk as she took care of their orders, trying to ignore her misbehaving heart—and what it implied. She was not attracted to this man. No way.

When Janice left, Nate claimed her spot directly across the counter, took the bag Lindsey offered and counted out his money. "So what gives with Jarrod?"

"What do you mean?"

"He has sad eyes."

The man had impressive observation skills. Then again, maybe that was essential for journalists.

She opened the cash drawer and put the money in the correct slots. "His father died a few months ago of a massive heart attack. Since then, Jarrod's grades have been slipping. I'm making progress with his math. Not so much with his reading and composition."

"Has he had any counseling?"

"His mother took him for a while. But no one's been able to rekindle his interest in school." She handed him his change, taking care not to touch his fingers as she dropped the coins into his large palm.

"That's a shame. He seems like a nice kid. But his situation is a recipe for wasted potential."

"Not if I can help it."

"I wish you luck." He picked up the bag. "With that, and with The Point. Your dad told me what happened last night."

"There are a lot of people in this town who will fight to save it."

"But money talks."

"Not always."

"Usually it triumphs over sentiment. My guess is it's a lost cause."

Her hackles rose at his cavalier response, and somewhere deep inside, Lindsey felt the stirring of an emotion that had long lain dormant.

Passion.

Not the kind she'd felt for Mark. That, she suspected, was dead forever. This was the kind of passion that had once animated her life and made her believe anything was possible, even when the odds were against her.

She gripped the edge of the counter and locked gazes with him. "That's a very negative attitude."

"It's the truth."

"So you think I should just stand aside and let this developer destroy The Point?"

He lifted one shoulder. "You probably won't be able to stop him, anyway. You could end up expending a lot of time and energy for nothing. It's just a falling down church, Lindsey. And that piece of land looks like a thousand other pieces of land along the coast."

"Then why did you come all the way back here to see it?" His shoulders stiffened, but she forged ahead despite the warning sign. "You must have feelings for the place. And some things are worth fighting for, no matter the odds. If you didn't believe that, why else would you risk your life covering news in a war zone?"

His eyes chilled. "It's a job. And I get paid a lot of money for doing it."

She stared at the man across from her, who suddenly felt like a stranger all over again. "You mean you don't care about the stories you write?"

He gave a taut shrug. "I care about the quality of my work. I won't turn in a shoddy piece."

"I'm not talking about grammar and punctuation and style rules. I'm talking about the impact your stories have on people's lives. And on public opinion."

The smile he gave her held no humor. "I'm not famous. Any impact I have is fleeting. One day my articles are in the paper, the next day that paper's lining a birdcage. What I write doesn't matter in the big scheme of things."

"Wow." She blinked. Was there anything left of the sensitive little boy she'd once known? "That's pretty cynical."

"I prefer the term realistic."

"If you don't think it matters, why do you do it?"

His lips flattened. "I happen to have a talent for writing. And it's a way to make a living."

"There are safer ways."

"Maybe I like the excitement."

"People don't put their lives on the line in battle zones for the sake of excitement. There must be some other reason."

He picked up the bag with the cookie. "Thanks for this."

End of conversation.

And she couldn't blame him. He hadn't come in here to be badgered. Who was she to call him to task, when she'd done little more than drift from day to day for the past three years?

As he turned away, she took a deep breath. "Nate…"

He hesitated. Angled back.

She folded her arms over her chest. "Look, I don't have any right to judge your choices. I'm sorry if I offended you."

"You didn't." The rigid line of his shoulders belied his words.

Gripping her upper arms, she studied him. When she spoke again, her quiet words seemed to surprise him as much as they did her. "So what happened to that soft-hearted little boy named Nathaniel I once knew?"

A muscle twitched in his cheek, and the sudden bleakness in his expression tightened her throat. "He grew up. And discovered it's a lot wiser to be tough than soft."

With that, he retreated to the coffee nook.

Thrown off guard by his candor, she had no idea how to respond.

Sixty seconds later, he reappeared, computer in one hand, cookie bag in the other. He nodded at her as he opened the door, but he didn't speak.

The bell jingled behind him, and she shifted around to watch him drive away. When at last she lost sight of his car, she sank onto the stool her father used, a hollow feeling in the pit of her stomach.

Regretting her critical comments.

And wondering if she'd ever see him again.

This trip wasn't turning out anything like he'd hoped.

Kicking a rock out of his path, Nate approached the chain that blocked access to The Point, vaulted over it and set off down the gravel road.

To be fair, he wasn't sure what he'd hoped to find here. A sense of peace, maybe. Answers. Welcome.

Home.

The welcome had been extended. But everything else had been elusive.

And he'd probably shot himself in the foot back there with Lindsey a little while ago. The shock on her face at his cynicism had been like a kick in the gut.

A rumble of thunder sounded in the distance, and Nate checked the sky. Dark clouds had moved in while he'd dumped his computer at the Orchid and called to check in at the *Tribune*. Fitting, considering his mood.

He covered the distance to the cliffs in record time, uncertain why he'd made the trek. The overgrown grounds and decaying chapel were one more reminder things had changed. That whatever happiness he'd once found here was as ephemeral as the mist rising from the crashing waves below.

The place was deserted. And this time, the bench was, too.

As he rounded the chapel and paused to look at the seat, he could picture the younger Lindsey sitting there the day they'd met, hair in two braids, binoculars glued to her eyes, a brown sack beside her.

She'd remained unmoving for so long he'd begun to wonder if she was a statue. And then she'd uttered an excited, "Yes!" and pumped a fist in the air.

Confused, he'd peered into the distance. But all he'd been able to see on that April day had been a vast expanse of water.

Not that he'd cared. He'd been too busy fighting back disappointment that someone had claimed his spot. The one he'd been coming to almost every day since he'd discovered it the first time he'd attended services here with his mother, two weeks before.

But just as he'd prepared to beat a quiet retreat, the girl had suddenly swung toward him, eyes shining. "Hey! You want to see the whales? There's a whole pod of them!"

That had been the start of a beautiful, if brief, friendship.

Now, as he strolled over to the bench, Nate reached

into his pocket and fingered the agate he'd found on one of their beach excursions. All these years, he'd never been without it—his one physical link to his happy months in Starfish Bay. A literal touchstone to his past.

As he ran his fingers over the smooth surface that had been polished by nature on the coarse sand of the beach below, it felt as familiar to his fingers as the keys of his laptop. He pulled it out and examined the translucent, inch-and-a-half diameter stone with its intricate white banding that created a pattern of circles, curves and wavy lines. Lindsey had told him it was a good one. She'd also told him the real beauty of agates lay inside, hidden from the world. And that it took a master cutter to reveal that beauty to its best advantage.

He'd liked that thought as a shy eleven-year-old who kept so much locked inside.

He still did.

Weighing the small stone in his hand, he drew in a lungful of the salt air. Despite what he'd told Lindsey, the plight of The Point and the chapel distressed him. If it was torn down, one more touchstone from his past would vanish forever.

Touchstone.

The word echoed in his mind.

Despite the dark clouds scuttling across the sky, Nate sat on the weathered concrete seat, the rhythm of the surf and the cry of the gulls a balm to his soul. People needed places like this to return to—or to discover for the first time. They needed links to places and peoples and things that helped define who they were, that reminded them of the experiences and relationships that had shaped them.

They needed touchstones.

Words began to form in his mind. Not the kind he

usually wrote. But compelling enough to induce him to pull out the notebook and pen he always carried and jot them down.

More followed.

He kept writing.

Nate had no idea how long he scribbled in his notebook. But he'd filled quite a few pages before the first drop of rain interrupted him.

He didn't stop, though. He couldn't. The words gushed forth, as unstoppable as a spring deep in the earth that works its way to the surface and suddenly breaks through to the light, the clear water sparkling in the sun.

Only when the rain picked up did he at last tuck the damp notebook back into his pocket and take off at a jog for the main road, more energized than he had been in a long while. Sure, he knew how to put words together, to create a compelling story, to manipulate emotions. But the words he'd just written were different.

They'd come from the heart.

And putting them on paper had made him feel good.

By the time he reached the main road, the rain had gone from a light shower to a steady downpour. He'd be soaked before he got to the Orchid.

But his heart felt lighter than it had in years.

And it lightened even more after he stepped inside his room and found a plastic-covered plate containing two cinnamon rolls on the desk, the "Glad you're here. Enjoy!" note signed by Genevieve.

He'd been adopted.

Nate hadn't shown his face at the Mercantile for three days. And his car had been missing from the

Orchid Motel parking lot whenever Lindsey had contrived a reason to drive by. She was beginning to think
he'd gone back to Chicago.

Not that it mattered. Despite their childhood friendship, which she barely remembered, they were strangers
now, with little in common. Their last conversation had
convinced her of that. And he was just passing through,
anyway.

Still, when she spotted Lillian pulling into the Mercantile parking lot, she decided to ask a few discreet
questions.

As the older of the two sisters approached the door
and set the bell jangling, Lindsey was struck, as always,
by their differences. While Genevieve was short and a
bit rounded, with white hair she always wore in a soft
chignon, Lillian was tall and spare, and her cropped
dark hair sported only a few streaks of gray even if she
was seventy.

"'Morning, Lillian."

"It is, indeed. I think that front has finally passed
through. It looks to be a glorious day. I believe I'll go
beachcombing this afternoon."

"Sounds like a fine idea. What can I help you with
today?"

"Pecans. After Genevieve started the waffle batter
this morning, she discovered she was low. I keep trying
to convince her to track inventory on the computer so
I can order the proper amounts. Instead, she leaves me
little notes scribbled on the back of café receipts instead." Sighing, she rolled her eyes. "Last time I ordered pecans, I couldn't read her handwriting and only
got half what she wanted. Result? I'm on an emergency
mission. Six people have ordered pecan waffles already.
Including our nice young guest from Chicago."

Nate was still in town.

Her spirits taking an uptick, Lindsey started toward the baking supplies. "We don't carry a lot of nuts. How many do you need?"

"Three pounds, if you have that much. She said that'll get her through."

"I haven't seen Nate around in the past few days." Lindsey picked up several eight-ounce packages and started back toward the counter. "I thought he might have gone back to Chicago by now."

"No. He paid a week in advance, so I expect he'll be around until Monday morning, at least." Lillian passed over her credit card as Lindsey rang up the purchase. "You're a lifesaver."

"Hardly." She handed her the receipt. "So how has he been keeping himself busy?"

Lillian chuckled. "Eating, for one thing. Never misses a meal, according to Genevieve, who keeps tabs on such things. Now if I could just get her to exhibit an equal interest in the computer."

"I don't think I'd hold my breath."

"Isn't that the truth." The older woman picked up her bag. "Well, I do know what our Chicago guest is doing this morning."

"What?"

With a grin, Lillian tucked the bag into the crook of her arm. "Visiting the Mercantile. He just pulled up. See you later."

Lindsey's pulse kicked up a notch, and she had to fight back an urge to run a brush through her hair and touch up her lipstick. Why should she care how she looked to Nate?

The bell jingled. Lillian paused inside the door to say a few words, and she heard the rumble of Nate's baritone response. Then he stepped inside and glanced toward her.

"Hi." She wiped her damp palms down her jeans and gave him a shaky smile.

"Hi." He didn't smile back as he lifted his laptop. "Email?"

He was still miffed at her. Served her right for being judgmental. "Help yourself."

"You sure? I don't want to take advantage of your hospitality."

"All of our customers are welcome to use the wireless."

He closed the door. But instead of turning left, toward the coffee nook, he strolled over to the counter.

Lindsey scrutinized his face as he approached. There was some subtle difference in him today. A little less tension in his features, perhaps? A more relaxed stance?

He set the computer on the counter. "I'd like to apologize."

She blinked. "I think that's my line."

"No. I walked out in the middle of our last conversation. That was rude."

"Maybe it was self-preservation. I overstepped. And I was the one who was rude." She grimaced and tucked her hair behind her ear. "I did that at the town council meeting the other night, too. I don't know what's come over me lately. I don't usually get worked up like that."

One side of his mouth hitched up. "You used to. I remember your eyes spitting fire the day we found that teenager tormenting a stranded seal on the beach. He was twice as big as you, but man, you gave him an earful. Once you scared him off, you made me help you roll the seal back to the water."

Her own lips lifted. She hadn't thought about that

day in years. "I guess I did come on a little strong. But that seal needed help. I couldn't stand by and do nothing."

"I always liked that about you. And I bet it helped make you a great teacher."

Warmth crept up her neck. "I pushed my students too hard sometimes, though. I hated to see wasted potential."

"Sometimes people need to be pushed."

She had a feeling he wasn't talking about her students anymore.

"So...truce?" He took his computer off the counter and held out his hand.

"Truce." She placed her hand in his, and he gripped it with his long, lean fingers, his touch warm and strong and somehow comforting.

He held it for a beat longer than necessary, his gaze locked on hers. When at last he released her, the floor seemed to shift a little. She groped for the counter, needing something solid to hang on to.

"I might be back for a cookie later. What's on the menu today?" He perused the dome.

"Oatmeal raisin."

"I don't remember your mom ever making those."

"She didn't. They were Mark's—my husband's— favorite." Nothing like a reminder of the tragedy that had brought her home to drop her back to earth with a thud.

His expression softened. "You still miss him a lot, don't you?"

"Every day." Her voice choked on the last word.

"In a way, I envy him."

Jolted, she frowned. "Why?"

"Enduring love is in short supply in today's world.

He was a lucky man to find it. Save me a cookie, okay?" With that, he continued toward the coffee nook.

As Lindsey watched him go, another little unwanted electric charge fluttered along her nerve endings. It wasn't attraction, though. Her heart belonged to Mark. She was just intrigued by this visitor from her past, who had secrets he'd hinted at but hadn't shared.

And attraction and curiosity were two very different things.

Absolutely.

Chapter Five

"**It** had been years since anyone lived in the di…'" Jarrod's halting voice faltered.

"Let's sound it out, okay?"

Letter by letter, Lindsey helped him work through the sounds until *dilapidated* emerged.

Nate tried to concentrate on his email, but the scene at the adjoining table in the coffee nook was more than a little distracting. Lindsey hadn't been exaggerating. Jarrod's reading skills were dismal.

"'…dilapidated house, except for rats and pi…'" He stopped again.

Lindsey went through the process again. Jarrod finally got the word.

"'…pigeons. Everyone in my class walked on the other side of the street when they passed, es…'"

Nate took a sip of coffee. This was downright painful.

The phone rang behind the counter, and Lindsey rose. "My dad had to run to the post office, Jarrod. You read ahead and work through the words while I answer that, then you can read it out loud when I come back."

The boy watched her go, gave the book a disgusted look, and heaved a loud sigh.

Nate leaned back in his chair and shifted toward him. "What are you reading?"

Shooting him a wary glance, Jarrod held up the book. Based on the somewhat eerie cover, it looked like the kind of suspenseful story an eleven-year-old boy would like.

"Any good?"

"I don't know. I hate reading. And writing."

"How come?"

"It's boring. And it's hard."

"It doesn't have to be either. I read and write every day in my job, and it's pretty exciting."

"Yeah?" Jarrod regarded him, clearly skeptical. "So what are you, a lawyer or something?"

"No. I write for a newspaper. I just got back from Afghanistan, writing stories about the war."

"Yeah?" The youngster's interest picked up. "Were you around the tanks and guns and everything?"

Nate's fingers tightened on the coffee cup. "Every day."

"That must have been cool."

"Most of the time it was scary."

"So why did you do it?"

Even kids were asking him that question now. "I like to write. And there were interesting stories to tell. But I've also been a lot of other places around the world, writing different kinds of stories. And I read a lot. Most of it on this." He tapped his laptop. "That's how I do some of my research. Do you use the computer very much?"

"When my mom lets me. I like playing games."

"You ever use it to look up stuff you're interested in?"

He wrinkled his nose. "Not unless they make us at school."

"Too bad. I'm getting ready to start on a story, and I could use some help with research. I'd even give an assistant a credit line." Nate frowned as the words left his mouth. What was that all about?

"You mean the person's name would be in the newspaper?" Another flicker of interest sparked in Jarrod's irises.

Okay, he was in now. He'd just have to wing it. "Yeah."

"What's the story about?"

Good question.

As he tried to come up with an answer, more unbidden words tumbled out of his mouth. "Children who lose one or both of their parents, and what that means in their lives."

Now where had *that* come from? He didn't want to write a story like that. It hit far too close to home. And considering how his face shuttered, Jarrod felt the same way.

Okay. Time to regroup. He didn't want to lose the boy.

On the other hand, researching that topic might help Jarrod work through his grief. But he'd have to feel comfortable with it—and with his mentor. Know he was in sympathetic company. And as far as Nate could see, there was only one way to accomplish that—even if it took him out of his comfort zone.

After a fortifying swig of coffee, he set the cup on the table. "I think it will be an important story, Jarrod.

And I know what it's like to go through that. I lost both my parents when I was a kid."

The boy's eyes widened. "Both?"

"Yeah. My mother died when I was eleven, and my dad didn't…couldn't take care of me after that. So I had to go live with a foster family. A year later my dad died."

"Wow. That must have been hard."

"It was. Sometimes it still is." Nate's voice hoarsened, and he cleared his throat.

The boy bowed his head and played with the edge of the book. "My dad died last winter. Right after Christmas."

"I'm sorry to hear that. But your mom's there for you, isn't she?"

"Yeah. She's cool. She tries to smile, and she takes me out for pizza every Friday. But I hear her crying at night sometimes, so I know she misses Dad a bunch, too. When he was alive, we always laughed a lot at our house. Now it's real quiet. And sad." The last few words were choked, and he swiped at his eyes with the sleeve of his sweatshirt.

Nate wished he could promise Jarrod things would get better. But they never had for him.

Then again, he hadn't had a mother to help him through the trauma.

As Nate searched for words of consolation, he glanced up to find Lindsey watching them from a few feet away. Her expression was enigmatic, but he had no trouble reading the surge of color that flooded her cheeks. She was embarrassed to have been caught eavesdropping.

"So how are you doing with the story?" Breaking

eye contact with him, she retook her seat across from her pupil.

Jarrod shot her a guilty look. "I didn't get very far. I was talking to him." He gestured toward Nate.

"It was my fault." Nate rested an elbow beside his computer on the small table. "We were discussing a business proposition." He directed his next comment to Jarrod. "Let me know if you're interested, okay?"

"Okay."

He and Lindsey went back to their book.

After fifteen more excruciating minutes of arduous reading, the bell over the front door jingled and a blonde woman, who looked to be in her late thirties, dashed in and headed straight for the coffee nook.

"Sorry." Her apology came out in a rush of breath as she pushed her windblown hair back from her face, the tremor in her fingers slight but noticeable. "There was an accident north of Eureka. Traffic was stopped both ways for twenty minutes. Hi, sweetie." She leaned down and kissed Jarrod on the top of his head.

"No problem, Cindy." Lindsey closed the book and passed it over to her student. "We needed a little extra time, anyway. I'll see you Wednesday, Jarrod."

"Okay." When he didn't say anything else, Cindy rested her hand on his thin shoulder and lifted an eyebrow. He sighed. "Thank you, Ms. Collier."

"You're welcome."

As Lindsey and his mother chatted for a moment, the youngster eased closer to Nate. "Maybe I could help you with your story. But I don't read real good yet. Or very fast."

Nate lowered his voice to match the boy's muted tone. "That's okay. I'm not in a hurry. I'll talk to Lindsey about it."

"Ready, Jarrod?" Cindy gave Nate a narrow-eyed look and tugged Jarrod closer.

"Yeah."

At the woman's protective behavior, Nate rose and held out his hand. If he wanted to have a chance to help the boy, he needed to make a positive impression on the mother. "Nate Garrison. I used to live here."

"We were friends years ago," Lindsey added, surprising him with her endorsement. "Nate's a journalist with the *Chicago Tribune*, here on vacation."

The woman's taut posture relaxed, and after a few pleasantries, she and Jarrod exited.

Before Lindsey left to relieve her father at the counter as she usually did after she finished with Jarrod, Nate broached the subject he'd discussed with the boy. She listened, brow furrowed, as he told her about the youngster's interest in his project.

"Are you really working on a story about children who've lost parents?"

"I am now."

"Why?"

Nate ran his fingers through his hair, then propped his fist on his hip. "You want the truth? I haven't a clue. The idea just popped out. It's obvious Jarrod's still dealing with a lot of issues and a lot of grief. If he finds out he's not alone, learns how others in his shoes feel and are coping, it might help him heal. I guess I recognized that at some subconscious level."

"Why do you care about Jarrod's problems? He's a stranger to you."

He shrugged. No use pretending Lindsey hadn't heard the background he'd shared with Jarrod. "I was in his shoes once. It would have meant a lot to me to have someone step in and try to make things better. Maybe I can do for him what no one ever did for me."

Lindsey studied him, her features softening. "And maybe you're not so cynical and jaded after all."

His neck warmed, and he turned away to retake his seat in front of his laptop. "Don't get your hopes up."

She ignored that. "I didn't know you'd lost your mother. Or been in foster care. I'm sorry."

Her tone was gentle, soothing him in a way he didn't deserve. Gritting his teeth, he stared at the geometric screen saver in front of him. "Don't be. It was my own fault."

Silence greeted that comment, and when he finally looked up he found Lindsey frowning down at him, her lower lip caught between her teeth.

Uh-oh. She was poised to get into some heavy stuff. And unlike the day of their reunion at The Point, he had no intention of encouraging her. He'd said too much already. "I have a proposition for you. About Jarrod."

For an instant he thought she was going to forge ahead with whatever questions were forming in her mind. But to his relief, the creases in her brow smoothed and she switched gears. "Okay."

"If his mother agrees to let him help me on this project, that could take the place of your reading lessons. Since my topic is a subject he's interested in, it might come easier for him. And I'll work it out so we know he's actually doing the reading and comprehending the text."

Lindsey pursed her lips and folded her arms across her chest. "I suppose it might be worth a try. I'm not getting anywhere with the books I've been offering, though most kids his age find them interesting."

"Most kids his age haven't lost a parent."

She conceded his point with a slight lift of one shoulder. "It might work, depending on how long you're planning to hang around. He wouldn't progress much in two or three sessions."

Truth be told, Nate had no idea how long he was going to stay. But he did know he wasn't close to being ready to go back yet.

"I can commit to two weeks. Beyond that...I'm not certain."

"Okay. That might be long enough to produce some results. I'll call Cindy tonight and run the idea by her. We could step up the classes while you're here, too—if you're willing. Meet four days a week instead of three."

"Fine by me." He pulled a notebook out of his pocket and jotted down a number on a blank page. "Why don't you call me after you talk to Jarrod's mother?" He ripped the sheet out and handed it over.

"Lindsey! You want to take over so I can go home and start dinner?" Jack's voice wafted over the shelving units that defined the coffee nook.

"I'll be there in a minute." She fingered the piece of paper. "This is a very nice gesture. Thanks for offering to help."

The warmth in her eyes reached deep inside him, thawing the chill that had long ago numbed his heart.

"It's no big deal. And it might not work."

"You know the old saying, it's the thought that counts. This one gets high marks."

With that, she swiveled around to answer her father's summons.

As she disappeared from view behind the shelves, Nate rested his elbows on the table and linked his fingers. He was glad Lindsey was touched by his gesture.

But a story on children losing a parent? What had he gotten himself into?

He had no doubt Clark Gunn, the features editor at the *Tribune*, would be interested in the piece. And it was possible that reading about other children whose parents had died would, indeed, help Jarrod find ways to cope with his loss.

But his gut also warned him he might be opening a can of worms from his own past that was better left undisturbed.

And his gut was rarely wrong.

"How about a second helping of those scalloped potatoes?" Genevieve paused beside Nate's table and smiled down at him. "You made short work of the first one. And everything else."

Nate checked out his plate. It was clean enough to bypass the dishwasher, thanks to his diligent efforts to sop up every last speck of gravy with one of Lillian's melt-in-the-mouth biscuits.

"I can't keep eating like this. I'll go home twenty pounds heavier."

"You could stand to gain a little weight."

That was true. He'd grown too lean in Afghanistan. But violence and gore had a way of killing a man's appetite. As did the *memory* of violence and gore. Since arriving in Starfish Bay, though, he'd been scarfing down every meal.

"Maybe. And you and your sister are doing your part. This was the best salisbury steak I ever ate. And the gravy…" He gave a satisfied sigh. "You two should have your own program on Food Network."

Genevieve beamed at him. "Flattery will get you everywhere. How would you like a piece of blackberry cobbler—on the house?"

Nate patted his stomach. "No room, I'm sorry to say. But I'll take a rain check."

"You've got it. Does that mean you'll be staying around a few more days?"

He gave her a sheepish look as he realized he'd only paid through last night. "I decided earlier today to hang around a little longer. Another couple of weeks, at least. Which means I owe you more money."

The older woman waved his comment aside. "You can settle up when you leave. You must be having fun, if you're staying longer."

Fun? Not quite the right word.

"Interesting would be a better way to describe it." He wiped his lips on his napkin and set the lavender cloth on the table, next to the paper placemat adorned with orchids.

"You've certainly been spending a lot of time at the Mercantile."

"They have Wi-Fi."

"Not to mention a pretty shopkeeper." Genevieve grinned. "Lindsey Collier is a real looker, as they used to say in my day. Before compliments like that were deemed politically incorrect."

Nate did his best to keep the flush on his neck from creeping any higher. "I remember her as a little girl with pigtails."

"She's all grown up now."

No kidding.

"That happens to all of us." He kept his tone conversational, though his pulse kicked up a notch as he pictured the gentle curve of her lips. "I used to be a skinny kid with smudged glasses."

"You grew up real fine, too." She leaned over and adjusted the bud vase that held a single silk orchid. "I hope you won't think I'm being too personal, but I've been wondering if there might be a wife or girlfriend or fiancée somewhere waiting for you."

Uh-oh. He knew what that gleam in Genevieve's eyes meant. Time for diversionary tactics.

"No. My job isn't conducive to any of the above. No one's waiting for me anywhere, except my boss. Besides, I'm not in the market for romance at this point in my life."

"Lindsey said the same thing while we were chatting after church yesterday." Genevieve exhaled and shook her head. "If you ask me, that girl needs to move on. Though I must say the pickings around here were slim until recently." She aimed a knowing wink in his direction.

Subtlety was clearly not Genevieve's forte—in decor or diplomacy. Might as well deal with this straight up.

"Genevieve, I'm only going to be here for a couple more weeks. And in case you have any romantic notions about a certain shopkeeper and the stranger in town, you need to know she didn't even remember me when I showed up at the Mercantile."

"That was then. This is now. And trust me, you've made quite an impression in the past week."

With a wink and a pat on the shoulder, she bustled off to chat with another customer.

Leaving Nate inexplicably lighter of heart, but also curious.

Just what had she and Lindsey talked about after church?

Chapter Six

Lindsey was impressed.

From the moment she'd turned Jarrod over to Nate in the coffee nook forty minutes ago, the two had been glued to the computer screen. Nate had walked his new assistant through some basic research principles and explained his expectations. Now he was helping him do a few preliminary searches. He'd even put a shortcut to a dictionary on his laptop, and had jotted down instructions for Cindy so she could do the same on their home computer. That way, when Jarrod got stuck, he could look up the word and the pronunciation.

Bottom line, Nate was treating the youngster like an adult colleague, and Jarrod was eating it up.

"He's good with the boy, isn't he?"

At her dad's comment behind her, she flushed. She'd tried to be discreet in her eavesdropping, but nothing much got past her father. "Seems to be. And it's kind of odd. As far as I know, he's never worked with children." She kept her face averted, hoping the heat in her cheeks would subside.

"Dealing with children is a natural skill. You either have it or you don't. And it takes a generous, selfless heart to do it well, whether you're a teacher or a parent. From what I've been picking up over there," he gestured to the coffee nook, "Nate's got the skill and the heart." Jack checked his watch. "As long as you're finished working with Jarrod for the day, do you mind if I cut out a little early? I'd like to weed the vegetable garden."

"No problem. It's been quiet, anyway."

"I expect things will pick up if that developer gets his way over at The Point. And he might."

Lindsey turned to him, furrowing her brow. "What have you been hearing?"

"Pros and cons. Seems to be about a fifty-fifty split. And there are strong opinions on both sides. I have a feeling next week's meeting will be lively—and standing room only."

She shoved her fists into the pockets of her jeans. "I wish I could think of some way to convince people it's the wrong thing to do."

"Are you sure it is?"

Her mouth dropped open. "How can you ask that? A development like that will ruin The Point!"

His expression gentled. "Not necessarily, Lindy. And it would benefit a lot of people. These are tough times. Even the Mercantile has been suffering for the past few years."

She knew that. The books didn't lie. She and her dad were getting by—but it was fortunate their needs were few and they were content with a simple life.

"Are you saying the end justifies the means?"

"You know better. I'm just saying maybe we should give this outfit a fair hearing."

A burst of laughter from the coffee nook drew her attention, and she glanced over. Jarrod was smiling, and for the first time since his father had died, she saw a spark of genuine joy in the youngster's eyes.

"Now that's a real positive sign." Her father indicated the duo. "Who'd have thought Nate's return would be a blessing for Jarrod? Interesting how God's plans manifest themselves. And speaking of the Almighty's plans, try not to worry about The Point, honey. He has plans for that place, too. I have absolute confidence in that."

As her father exited and she took her place behind the counter, Lindsey didn't doubt the truth of his words. She, too, was certain God had plans for The Point.

But she wasn't at all certain she would agree with them.

"Save me a cookie, okay, Lindsey?" Nate paused on his way out the door, surveying the line of three customers at the counter and the dwindling number of cookies under the dome. "I have to take a call from my editor and cell reception in here is marginal."

"Sure." Lindsey waved at him as she tucked the last item in Susan Peroni's canvas shopping tote.

"Dennis will be sending out the agenda for next week's meeting by Friday. You'll be there, I assume." Susan tugged the bag toward her across the counter.

"Of course. Along with most of the residents, from what I've been hearing."

The mayor sighed. "I just hope we can fit everybody in the town hall. We haven't had this much interest in a building issue since Jaz wanted to open his biker bar in the abandoned gas station on the other side of town. You weren't here then, were you?"

"No. But Dad kept me in the loop."

"A lot of people were against it. But look how well that turned out."

Lindsey clamped her lips together and busied herself at the cash drawer. The mayor *would* bring that up. The so-called biker bar, far from being the den of iniquity many residents had feared, was a family-friendly spot that served burgers and held dart tournaments for charity. And Jaz, his ever-present cheery smile neutralizing his scary tattoos, had become a model citizen of Starfish Bay.

"The Point is different, Susan."

The woman slung her purse over her shoulder and hefted her shopping bag. "I don't disagree with you. I love The Point, too. I also love this town. But we're facing some tough fiscal decisions, as the council well knows. No one wants Mattson Properties to destroy a natural resource, but if we cut them off without a hearing, aren't we being negligent in our civic duty? Not to mention unfair?"

There was only one answer to the question her dad had also raised, and Lindsey refused to voice it. "It's a moot point now, anyway. The special meeting is scheduled. They'll get their hearing." She looked over the woman's shoulder. "Hi, Hank. Did you find everything you need?"

"I did." The spry Starfish Bay octogenarian edged out the mayor, who got the hint and moved aside. "Hello, Susan. Talking about the meeting, I see. Well, Molly and I will be there, too."

"The more, the merrier." With one last sigh, the mayor exited.

By the time Lindsey waited on Hank and got an earful about why the development was a bad idea, then listened to Dennis Simms's wife talk about what a boon the development would be for their fishing camp, the stirrings of a headache were beginning to pulse in her temples.

After setting aside a cookie for Nate, she dampened a sponge in the back room, then checked out the coffee nook. Sure enough, the two tables vacated a little earlier by the teen crowd were littered with cookie crumbs and empty soda cans.

Once she'd straightened up their mess, she balanced the cans in the crook of her arm and surveyed Nate's table. It was free of clutter except for his open laptop, but a shriveled leaf on the golden pothos she'd carted back from Sacramento three years ago caught her attention.

As she leaned over to snag it, her elbow caught the edge of his screen, pushing it back. Juggling the cans in her arm, she readjusted it, glancing at the document that replaced the screen saver.

Two words jumped out at her.

The Point.

Intrigued, she scanned the text.

It wouldn't mean much to anyone else, this little patch of headland on the northern California coast. It looks like hundreds of other headlands, more scenic than some, not as scenic as most. Passing motorists might not even notice it as they zip by on Highway 101, their focus instead on the quaint town of Starfish Bay.

Yet The Point, as it's known to residents, is a touchstone for many. A place that helps define their town—and their hearts. An anchor in the turbulent sea of life. A repository of memories, exerting a pull strong enough to call home a prodigal son.

But this tiny piece of real estate is threatened, along

with the small chapel atop it that has offered solace and hope for decades. And if they disappear, there will...

"That's a private document."

At Nate's chilly tone, Lindsey jerked away from the computer screen. The soda cans slipped from her grasp and clattered to the floor.

As she bent to gather them up, heat flooded her cheeks. She'd been so engrossed in his words she'd missed the warning jingle of the bell over the door. "I'm sorry. I didn't mean to snoop. The reference to The Point caught my eye."

Instead of responding, Nate brushed past her and snapped the computer shut. When she stood, cans once again tucked into the crook of her arm, he'd slid it into its case and taken out his car keys. The taut line of his lips wasn't promising, but it couldn't hurt to try one more apology.

"Nate, I'm sorry."

"How much did you read?"

"Just a couple of paragraphs."

His fingers clenched on the handle of the case, and his blue eyes were cold as a Nordic glacier. "Where's the next closest spot with Wi-Fi?"

Her stomach twisted. "Crescent City."

She thought about apologizing again, but she'd already made two attempts. No reason to think he'd soften on a third try. And she couldn't fault him for being irritated at her for trespassing into private territory.

He started toward the exit, and she trailed after him. "Will you be back to help with Jarrod?"

Hand on the door, he angled toward her. "I always honor my commitments."

Somehow, that didn't surprise her. "Do you still want your cookie?"

"No." He turned his back on her and pushed through to the outside, flinging his final words over his shoulder. "I'm not hungry anymore."

The door banged shut behind him, the bell overhead sounding far too cheery as it announced his departure.

For a few seconds, Lindsey remained where she was. Then she trudged over to the counter, deposited the cans in the recycle bin, and watched through the window as he spun out of the parking lot in a churn of gravel.

Man, she'd really hit a nerve.

She climbed onto the stool, set her elbow on the counter and propped her chin in her hand. If he'd been working on an article for the *Tribune* about the war, she doubted he'd have reacted as strongly to her faux pas. But what she'd read had sounded more like a journal.

Cringing, she thought about how she'd feel if anyone read the diary she'd kept after Mark's death, at a grief counselor's suggestion. Not pleased, that's for sure. Those gut-wrenching thoughts had been torn from deep in her psyche. She wouldn't want her father to read them, let alone a virtual stranger. If Nate's piece contained even a smidgen of that soul-baring angst, it was no wonder he'd been so upset.

Yet her regret was tempered by a sudden rush of warmth for the man who'd mere days ago reacted with such cynicism to her vow to fight for The Point. Though he'd professed indifference, it seemed he was as unhappy about the potential loss as she was.

Too bad she couldn't persuade him to use his obvious literary talents to help save it.

But as she gazed out the window, where the dust was

at last settling after his hasty departure, she figured that was about as likely as Lillian convincing Genevieve to embrace the computer age.

Once again, he'd blown it.

Nate deposited his laptop on the bed in his room at the Orchid and raked his fingers through his hair. Last week he'd walked out of the Mercantile when Lindsey had probed a little too deep about why he put himself in the line of fire on the battlefield, asking questions that made him uncomfortable. Questions he'd never dwelt on—or answered—for himself.

Today he'd repeated that performance.

So much for hoping to reconnect with his childhood friend. At this point, she probably thought he was a first-class jerk.

Then again, didn't he have a right to be angry about her intrusion into his personal material? The piece on The Point had been meant for his eyes only. And it had served its purpose. Putting his feelings about the place into words had been cathartic. Had helped him begin to understand what had driven him to return here after all these years.

He shouldn't have left it on his screen when he'd gone out to take the call from his editor, though. If he hadn't, Lindsey would never have read it.

And what exactly had she read?

He sat on the bed, booted up his computer again and scrolled to the section that had been on display before he'd shut his computer at the Mercantile and stormed out.

A quick skim was reassuring. It wasn't as bad as he'd expected. The part where he talked about the vague yearning that had driven him back to this touchstone from his childhood, where he confessed that he'd held onto a vision of The Point—and Starfish Bay Chapel—during those first lonely weeks in foster care, and while he'd watched soldiers die around him in Afghanistan, came later.

Meaning he'd overreacted. She hadn't seen anything too revealing.

Too bad.

Nate frowned. What was that little echo of regret all about? And why did he feel a vague sense of disappointment?

Suddenly restless, he rose and crossed the room. He couldn't see The Point from his window. But it was comforting to know it was there, beyond the trees—along with the chapel and the bench where he'd spent so many happy hours. Material objects that linked him to the ephemeral—memories, joy, hopes, friendship.

Lindsey understood that. The Point was a touchstone for her, too.

And she was also a touchstone for him. A connection to a short sojourn in his life when hopes were high and all was right with the world. An idyllic time never since repeated.

Could that account for his surge of disappointment moments ago? He'd thought he'd come cross country to see The Point, had hoped the journey would help him get a handle on the issues that had been festering in his subconscious for years. But he'd known as soon as he'd laid eyes on Lindsey that she was a key to his journey, too. That reconnecting with her was important. Necessary.

Yet he'd been putting up roadblocks with her every step of the way. Fighting off every foray she made into his personal life. Backing away or reacting with anger when she got too close, like today.

And he knew why.

Propping a shoulder against the window frame, Nate inhaled a long, slow breath. He'd told Jarrod in their first conversation that he'd sometimes been scared in Afghanistan. Yet sharing his past with Lindsey—and taking a hard look at it himself—would require even more courage than facing bullets on the battlefield.

Because truth be told, the enemy within frightened him more.

"That's exactly the kind of information I need, Jarrod. And you've culled through and highlighted the most pertinent sections. Excellent work."

Passing the coffee nook with the special-order shovel she'd retrieved from the back room for a customer, Lindsey checked on the duo seated behind Nate's computer. Jarrod was beaming under the man's praise, and as Nate looked toward her, he smiled.

That was a positive sign. She hadn't exchanged more than a few words with him when he'd arrived for Jarrod's lesson, but he seemed friendlier today. He must have gotten over yesterday's hissy fit.

She continued to the counter and propped the shovel against the edge. "Here you go, Sam." She rang up the purchase, thanked the man for his business, and settled down to work on some notes for the town council meeting.

Except her mind was more on the man sitting a few yards away than on the plight of The Point.

After their rocky parting yesterday, she'd spent an hour on the internet, pulling up stories with Nate's byline from the *Tribune* archives. Hoping they'd offer her a little more insight into the man whose presence continued to unsettle her. And she hadn't felt in the least guilty reading those articles. They were public record, after all.

She'd learned a lot, too. Not just about his considerable skill with words, but about the man. His stories were an intriguing mix of contradictory emotions, and many had an underlying theme of courage in the face of desperation and despair. The profiles he'd done of troops under fire revealed soldiers who were often searching for meaning in their missions, yet who served with valor despite their doubts and fear.

Based on the brief snippet she'd read in his piece on The Point, the search for meaning was a recurring theme in both his professional and personal work.

Which led her to wonder if that was the reason for his journey to Starfish Bay. Was he on a quest, searching for meaning in his own life?

The bell over the door jingled, and she dropped the pen she'd been tapping against the blank sheet of paper.

Cindy entered, glanced toward the coffee nook, and joined her at the counter.

"The other day I was late. Today, I'm too early." The woman blew out a breath and massaged her forehead. "I can't seem to get my timing right anymore."

At the glint of moisture in Cindy's eyes, Lindsey's heart contracted. "Hey, trust me. Things will get better. Bit by bit, day by day. It's just really hard in the beginning." And even after three years, in the lonely hours of the night, though she left that unsaid.

"That's what I keep telling myself. At least I'm beginning to adjust to the nine-to-five world again. And I'm lucky Ruth agreed to watch Jarrod during the summer and shuttle him here for his sessions with you. She's been a godsend."

"No arguments there. I don't know how she does it, with four children of her own, but she always finds time to help those in need. She was there for me after I moved back, too. She invited me and Dad to dinner every couple of weeks and encouraged me to run for the town council. Plus, she stopped in here every few days to chat."

"That sounds like Ruth." As Cindy checked her watch, she leaned back to peer around the shelving. "Looks like they're still hard at it over there. You know, I couldn't get Jarrod off the computer last night. And he was so busy copying and pasting articles for Nate he didn't want to go to bed. Here's the best part, though— he wanted to talk about some of the things he'd read. He opened up even more than when he was seeing the grief counselor."

"That's wonderful, Cindy."

"It's a start, anyway. I don't know how long your friend is planning to hang around, but as far as I'm concerned, it can't be long enough." Cindy shifted a bulging satchel from one hand to the other. "Well, I guess I better break up the party over there. I don't want to overstay our welcome."

Five minutes later, as Cindy and Jarrod exited, Lindsey took a deep breath and walked toward the nook. Time to put her appeasement plan into action.

As she stepped into his line of sight, Nate motioned her over. "Take a look at this."

She circled around the table until she was beside him, then leaned down to see the screen. As the subtle scent of his aftershave wafted her way, she closed her eyes.

"Pretty amazing, huh?"

Yeah. Amazing.

Oh, wait. He was talking about something on the computer screen.

She opened her eyes and forced herself to focus on the text. Several sentences had been highlighted in yellow, and she tried to switch gears, to grasp the significance of what she was seeing.

Fortunately, Nate came to her rescue. "The only way I could be certain Jarrod was reading the material—and comprehending it—was to ask him to highlight passages he thought were important. And for a first go-round, he's done a remarkable job. Not only did he find relevant information, he did a great job picking out the most important parts."

Lindsey took a closer look, scanning the highlighted sentences. "You're right. I'm impressed. Cindy said she had to persuade him to go to bed last night because he was so into this."

"That's what we were after." As Nate leaned back, the hair near his temple brushed her cheek.

She straightened up and took a quick step away as her heart did a disturbing little skip.

He fixed those appealing blue eyes on her. "About yesterday, Lindsey. I'm sorry I overreacted."

The perfect setup to extend her olive branch of friendship. "And I'm sorry I read your private material. In fact, I was hoping to make amends by inviting you down to The Point after dinner for some whale watching. I'll supply the binoculars and chocolate chip cookies."

He shot her a surprised look. Had he seen through her ruse? Did he know this wasn't whale-watching season? Most non-residents didn't.

But then he smiled, dispelling those fears. "Now there's an invitation I can't refuse. Just name the time."

"Why don't I meet you at the access road about seven?"

"Could we take the trail from town instead? For old time's sake?"

"Sure. Do you remember where it starts?"

Twin creases appeared on his brow. "Behind the place that used to sell souvenirs—now a dental office?"

"Very good." The bell over the door jingled and she walked toward it. "Duty calls."

"Hey, thanks for the invitation."

She risked a quick glance over her shoulder. The warmth in his gaze played havoc with her equilibrium, but she did her best to maintain a conversational tone. "No problem. See you later."

Then she beat a hasty retreat.

Safely behind the counter once more, Lindsey tried to ignore the little buzz zipping through her. The kind that had nothing to do with friendship—and everything to do with attraction. Like it or not.

And she didn't like it.

She'd given her heart to Mark years ago. As far as she was concerned, it was still his—and would be long after her childhood friend accomplished whatever it was he'd come here to do and returned to his real life.

And despite the gyrations of her pulse in his presence, despite the traitorous tingle of electricity his cobalt eyes could generate, she had no intention of offering Nate anything more than friendship.

Chapter Seven

Nate watched Lindsey stride down the single-file path ahead of him toward The Point, the breeze ruffling her hair, her confident gait in marked contrast to the nervousness she'd exhibited when he'd shown up at the trailhead five minutes ago.

It didn't take a genius to figure out why she was on edge.

This excursion wasn't about whales. Wrong season. It was about attraction. She was feeling the charge that detonated every time they were together just as strongly as he was.

But he suspected that in Lindsey's mind, it was the wrong season for that, too.

The question was, would it be fair to try and convince her otherwise, given his temporary status in Starfish Bay?

His hormones said yes.

His conscience said no.

But that debate would have to wait. They'd reached The Point.

As they emerged from the woods, Nate lengthened his stride until they were side by side. The sun was still high in the sky, but it had begun its descent toward the horizon, the bright white light of day giving way to a more golden hue that suffused the chapel with a warm, flattering glow.

Lindsey's step slowed as she gazed at the structure. "I can still picture it the way it looked on my wedding day. We hung huge wreaths of wildflowers on both of the front doors, with different colored ribbons trailing down that danced in the breeze. It was beautiful."

At her soft comment, he looked over at her. Though the hint of a smile played at her lips, her wistful tone tugged at his heart. "Memories like that are why touch-stones are important."

She directed her attention to him, clearly surprised he'd broached that topic, given his reaction yesterday.

He was surprised, too.

Clearing his throat, he gestured toward the bench and started forward again. "Shall we?"

She fell in beside him, her expression pensive as they crossed the weed-covered ground and settled on the stone seat. After putting the white bag of cookies between them, she pulled the binoculars from their case and held them out to him.

Playing along with her charade, he lifted them and scanned the undulating blue sea. No whales. Surprise, surprise.

"Looks pretty quiet out there."

"Whale-watching takes patience."

"I remember. In the meantime, how about one of those cookies you promised?"

She fished one out of the bag and passed it to him.

He lowered the binoculars and took a bite. The chips were soft and gooey, the cookie slightly warm. "Did you just make these?"

A faint tinge of pink appeared on her cheeks as she tugged the binoculars from his grasp and pressed them to her eyes. "We sold out at the Mercantile. And I never break my promises."

Savoring the cookie, he watched her, just as he'd done twenty-five years ago. In the old days, he'd thought of her as strong. Indomitable. Courageous. His opinion hadn't changed. She might have lost the man she'd loved, but she was carrying on. Doing what had to be done. Trusting in a greater authority—as had the soldiers he'd interviewed on the battlefield.

Except he had a feeling her greater authority outranked even a five-star general.

"So do you still go to church every Sunday?"

At the out-of-the-blue question, her posture stiffened. "I try. It doesn't always happen." She kept the binoculars glued to her face.

"Your family never missed a Sunday when I lived here."

"Things change."

"Including God?"

She slowly lowered the binoculars and turned to him with a frown. "That sounds like something Reverend Tobias would have said."

Yeah, it did. Was it possible the man had spoken similar words to him, once upon a time? Funny they would surface after all these years.

Nate brushed the cookie crumbs off his fingers. "He and I had quite a few talks in this very spot. Maybe some of what he said stuck."

"I take it you've parted ways with God?"

He lifted a shoulder. "Let's just say I haven't seen much evidence of His presence in my life."

She lifted one heel to the bench, wrapped her arms

around her leg and rested her chin on her knee as she looked toward the horizon. "Yeah. I hear you. But He's still around. Still listening. It just takes a while sometimes for His voice to get through. Or so my dad is always reminding me." She sighed, then angled her head toward him, cheek on knee. "That's one of the reasons I keep coming out here, where His voice was always strongest. Hoping to hear it again. More evidence of the value of touchstones."

As he reached over to take another cookie, the folded sheets of paper in his shirt pocket crinkled. Reminding him of their presence. And of the compelling sense of urgency that had pulled him back to this spot, to the one place where, for a brief moment in time, life had made sense. The place where he'd hoped to find answers. Absolution. Hope. So far, that search had been a bust.

Perhaps because the key to it lay in a person, not a place.

In Lindsey, if he could find the courage to open his heart.

Pulling his hand back from the cookies, he lifted it to his pocket. Fingered the sheets of paper. Eased them out.

God, please help me do this!

The silent plea was out before he could stop it. Odd. It had been years since he'd spoken to the Lord. Yet here, in the shadow of the chapel where Reverend Tobias had ministered with such kindness, compassion and deep, abiding faith, it felt right.

Opening the sheets with fingers that weren't quite steady, Nate swallowed past the sudden tightness in his throat. "Speaking of touchstones…you read some of this yesterday. I thought you might like to read the rest." He held it out to her, across the bag of chocolate chip cookies. Across the years.

She glanced at it, then gave him a wary look. "Why the sudden change of heart?"

The truth—that he thought she was as special now as she'd been twenty-five years ago, and that in a mere handful of days he felt closer to her than anyone else in his life—might scare her off. So he settled for a portion of the truth.

"Since you love The Point, I think you might appreciate it. And I trust you to keep the personal stuff to yourself."

After one more assessing sweep, she took the sheet, shifted back toward the open sea, and began to read.

No more than a few paragraphs into the document, Lindsey realized that Nate had given her an amazing gift.

Not only was the piece evocative, eloquent and thought-provoking—it also told her much about the grown-up version of the little boy who long ago had shared this bench with her.

This was a man who asked the hard questions and didn't settle for easy answers. A searcher who, like Carl Sandburg, recognized that life was like an onion—you peel it off one layer at a time, and sometimes you weep. A man who understood that true value wasn't measured in dollars and cents, but in treasures of the heart.

And a man who was wrestling with demons hinted at here, but not fully revealed.

When she reached the last paragraph, she read it twice.

This time next year, in the name of progress, The Point may exist only in memory. The chapel that com-

pelled a wayward soul to make a cross-country trek may have vanished. The world won't end, of course. Or perhaps even notice the loss. But it will be less rich in all the ways that matter.

As she finished, Lindsey took a deep breath. There were references here she didn't understand—like soldiers dying around him on a battlefield—but one thing was very clear. He'd offered her a window to his soul. And she was honored.

But she was also scared.

A man didn't do that unless he liked you. A lot.

Too much.

She lifted her head and looked at him. He was watching her, his studiously neutral expression giving no hint of his feelings.

Taking her time, she folded the sheets of paper, unsure how to deal with Nate's deeper motivations for sharing this piece. Better to focus on the piece itself for now. Later, she'd work through the personal implications.

"This is amazing."

Nate attempted a smile, but couldn't seem to get his lips to cooperate. "It's not my usual style."

"Maybe it should be." She fingered the document. "You've captured exactly the reasons why The Point is worth saving."

"That's not why I wrote it."

"I understand that." She passed the sheets back to him, ignoring the warmth of his fingers when they brushed hers. "But you have an incredible ability to touch people with your words. I saw that in your war stories, too, but this is…"

"What war stories?"

Oops. She hadn't intended to let that slip.

She shifted on the bench and clasped her hands in her lap, over the binoculars. There was no honest way out of that little gaffe. "After the snippet I read yesterday, I was interested to see what else you'd written. So I went online and pulled up some of your articles. There was some powerful writing in there."

He tucked the touchstones piece back in his pocket. "Thanks."

At his cryptic response, her stomach knotted. She was blowing this. Big time. After his reaction yesterday when he'd found her in front of his computer screen, it was clear Nate wasn't accustomed to baring his soul. Today's venture outside his comfort zone deserved more than a commentary on writing skills.

"Nate." Pulse pounding, she untwisted her fingers and reached over the bag of cookies to touch his forearm. "I'm honored you offered to let me read the piece. But can I tell you the truth? That gesture makes me a little nervous."

His eyebrows rose. "Why?"

She moistened her lips. "Because it's the kind of thing people only share with someone they care about a lot. And trust."

His gaze didn't waver. "That's true."

Suspicion confirmed. He liked her too much.

"I appreciate that. And I like you a lot, too. It's nice to reconnect with a friend after all this time." She gave a subtle emphasis to the word *friend*. "As long as we're both clear about the status of our relationship."

"There's a connection between us, Lindsey. I know you feel it as much as I do."

At the intensity in his eyes, and his unexpected candor, her breath caught in her throat. "It's been twenty-five years. We're almost strangers."

"You don't feel like a stranger." He rested one hand on the stone seat beside the bag of cookies, his fingers a whisper away from her leg.

She eased away on the pretext of making room beside her for the binoculars. Yet she couldn't deny the truth. The quarter-of-a-century gap in their relationship did seem to be imploding. She felt as comfortable in Nate's presence as she had when they'd been kids—except for the unwelcome complication of grown-up hormones.

She cleared her throat. "But you won't be here long. Don't you think it would be better to keep things simple?"

"Probably."

"Absolutely." Before he could challenge her more definitive response, she nodded to the papers in his pocket. "So if that's not your usual style, why did you write it?"

He hesitated for an instant, and she held her breath, praying he'd respect the boundary she'd set. Only when he retracted his arm did she exhale.

"I don't know. I didn't plan to. I came out here the other night after we had our little discussion about The Point, and the words started flowing. Even I didn't know how strongly I felt about this place until then."

"It's a beautiful piece. The kind that would resonate even with people who've never heard of The Point. Everyone has touchstones." She caught her lower lip between her teeth as an idea began to germinate. Dare she broach it? "I know you wrote that piece for yourself, but you have such a talent…a piece like that could touch a lot of hearts. Generate support for saving The Point."

He stared at her, and she read the shock in his eyes—before they narrowed and grew cold. "Is that why you asked me out here tonight? To try and convince me to go public with this, based on the small part you read?" He tapped his pocket.

"No! I never intended to bring it up again until you offered to let me read the whole thing. The idea just occurred to me. You have a fabulous gift with words. If The Point disappears, won't you feel terrible, knowing you might have been able to help save it?"

He rose abruptly and moved a few steps closer to the edge of the cliff, fists clenched at his sides. "I don't need you to lay more guilt on me. I've got plenty already."

"I'm not trying to make you feel guilty." She rose, too.

"No?" He faced her, his expression as turbulent as the water crashing against the rocks below them. "It sure sounded that way."

"Nate…" She held up her hands, palms toward him. "I don't want to fight with you again. But I think people who've been given a talent like yours have an obligation to use it for good. Like you did on the battlefield, when you told those soldiers' stories with such insight and compassion. This is just a different kind of battlefield."

"It's not my battle." He folded his arms over his chest. "I don't live here anymore."

"But the place is important to you. And to me. And to a lot of other people."

A muscle in his cheek jerked and he shook his head. "It's not my battle."

"It could be. Why are you afraid of letting people get a glimpse of the man behind that tough, ace-combat-reporter image? From what I've seen, he's a great guy."

"There's a lot you haven't seen." He returned to the

bench, picked up the binoculars and shoved them back in the case. "You ready to call it a night?"

"No."

"I am." He left the binoculars on the bench and started toward the gravel road that would take him back to the Orchid.

Lindsey planted her hands on her hips and huffed out a breath. Why did they end up fighting every time they got together? Whatever the reason, though, it was more proof they shouldn't get involved.

"Fine." Fuming, she grabbed the bag of cookies with one hand and the binoculars with the other, then circled the bench and stalked toward the path that led back to the heart of town. Ten feet into her trek, however, she paused to call out to his retreating back. "But you know what? I think you're being really selfish!"

To her surprise, he stopped. Turned. Anger simmered in his eyes, and she could feel the tension radiating from him even across the dozen yards that separated them.

Yet in the depths of those blue irises, she also saw hurt.

Her throat tightened, and the pressure built behind her own eyes. If she could, she'd take back that childish comment. Nate wasn't selfish. Far from it. His patient work with Jarrod proved that. But it was too late to retract the words.

And far too late to salvage the mess she'd made of this so-called appeasement outing—much as she wished she could.

Nate glared at Lindsey, equal parts guilt and fury nipping at the edges of his control.

Retreat or continue the fight?

No contest.

He never walked away from a fight.

Squaring his shoulders, he marched back to her. "How can you say I'm selfish? I've put myself in the line of fire for years, covering stories too risky for most reporters to sign on for."

"I know. Look, I got a little—"

He cut her off. "Let me tell you something. I've spent a lot of my life tilting at windmills, putting myself on the line exposing corruption, graft, dirty politics and the horrors of war. And along the way, I've also tried to pay tribute to the valor and courage I've witnessed. A lot of it in Afghanistan. It ate at my gut to watch good men die. Better men than me. Do you know what it's like to lie there, too stunned to move, too stunned to help, and watch someone bleed to death an arm's reach away? Do you have any idea what it feels like to be that helpless? To know that…"

Lindsey swayed, and the harsh words died in his throat as her pallor, her taut features, and the sudden anguish in her eyes registered.

The anger drained out of him.

"What's wrong?" He gripped her arms to steady her.

Instead of responding, she jerked out of his grasp, stumbled back a couple of steps, and lost her balance.

He lunged, grabbing her just in time to keep her from falling backwards. Shudders rippled through her, and he tightened his grip, his alarm ratcheting up. "Tell me what's wrong."

Ignoring his request, she yanked free, turned and took off for the path to town, dropping the bag of cookies as she fled.

What in the world was going on?

He didn't have an answer to that question. But he

didn't intend to let her run away without getting one. Though they'd both lost their tempers, anger didn't explain her sudden distress.

She had a head start by the time he took off after her, but she was no match for his long legs. In fifteen seconds he was beside her, his hand on her arm, tugging her to a stop.

"Lindsey, wait. Talk to me, okay?"

She dropped her chin, but she couldn't hide the tears streaming down her cheeks, her heaving chest or her silent sobs.

At her traumatized face, his stomach twisted. "Hey, come on." He gentled his voice, trying for a soothing tone. "We're old friends, remember? Even if we do fight a lot. Tell me what's wrong."

"Let me go." She tried to pull free.

"No. I can't let you leave like this. Tell me how I can help."

"You c-can't. N-no one can."

With a sudden jerk, she broke his hold on her arm. She twisted away and attempted to flee again, but he grabbed her around the waist, his hand pressed against the small of her back.

Against something hard.

Something that felt a lot like a…gun?

His childhood friend—the one who rescued stranded seals—carrying a lethal weapon?

It didn't compute.

"Lindsey?" He stared at her, his fingers locked on the compact object tucked inside the back of her jeans. "Is that a gun?"

With one more hard wrench, she pulled free and tore off for the woods, her hair streaming behind her.

Too stunned to follow, he watched until the forest swallowed her up.

Lindsey had a gun.

Why?

Shoving his fingers through his hair, Nate turned toward the church, silhouetted in front of the setting sun and jammed his fists in his pockets. Nothing about this trip had been easy. He'd come here looking for answers. For a return to a simple life where all the pieces fit. Instead, he'd found more questions. Knotty complications. Puzzles with missing pieces.

As he slowly retraced his route toward the gravel road, he passed the abandoned bag of chocolate chip cookies on the neglected lawn. He bent to pick it up, hefting it in his hand. Once upon a time, a chocolate chip cookie and a glass of milk had gone a long way toward solving life's problems. Not so anymore.

But he had other problem-solving resources at his disposal these days, at least when it came to Lindsey. He'd been curious about her past since he'd arrived in Starfish Bay, but he'd waited, hoping at some point she might share it with him. That hadn't happened.

Now it was time to take matters into his own hands.

And before this day was out, he intended to use his best investigative skills to see if he could ferret out the trigger for the dramatic end to their contrived whale-watching session.

Chapter Eight

"Everything okay, honey?"

Lindsey tucked her hair behind her ear and wrapped the fingers of both hands around her cup of tea. "Sure."

Her father eased into a chair across from her at the kitchen table. "I thought you were going out to The Point with Nate."

"I did."

He checked his watch. "Fast trip."

"It was a little windy."

"Never stopped you from enjoying a sunset out there before, near as I can recall."

At his speculative expression, she took a sip of her tea. "I saw some storm clouds gathering on the horizon, too." True enough. Though they'd been far too distant to justify cutting short a sunset show.

"Hmm." Her father rose. "Think I'll have some coffee."

As he puttered about the kitchen, Lindsey prayed he'd let the subject drop.

"So did you and Nate have a fight?"

She closed her eyes. So much for that hope.

"Why would I fight with him? We're practically strangers."

"You don't act like strangers."

She shot him a cautious look as he finished measuring instant coffee into a mug and filled it with water. "What's that supposed to mean?"

"I've seen the way you two look at each other when you think I'm not watching." He set the mug in the microwave and pressed the beverage button. "A person would have to be dead not to notice the sparks flying between you two."

Her cheeks warmed, and she dipped her chin to hide the telltale flush. She might have felt the vibes, but she'd hoped no one else had.

"He hasn't even been back two weeks, Dad. Isn't this conversation a little premature?"

"Is it?"

"Yes. Besides, I'm not in the market for sparks."

"Maybe you should be."

She shot him a startled glance. "How can you say that? I still love Mark."

"And you always will. That doesn't mean you can't love someone else, too."

The microwave pinged, giving Lindsey a few seconds to try and regroup as her father retrieved his coffee.

"You're feeling guilty about being disloyal to Mark, aren't you?"

She stifled a sigh. How had they gotten into this conversation, anyway?

"Dad…" She leaned toward him, tightening her grip on her mug as he sat. "I haven't seen Nate in twenty-five years. He'll be gone in a week or two. It's a moot point."

"No, it's not. I've been thinking about this for a while, long before Nate came back to town. You're too young to spend the rest of your life alone, Lindy. You should be sharing a house with a husband, not a father. Raising a family. Living. Loving. Mark was a wonderful man. One of the most unselfish people I ever met. And because he was unselfish, I know he wouldn't want you to waste your life grieving. So for the past year, I've been asking the good Lord to bring a new man into your life. Then along comes Nate. Your old friend. Seems more than coincidence to me."

Lindsey stared at him. "You've been praying that I find a new man?"

"It's a father's job, especially when a mother's not there to do it."

For a long moment, she studied him. "You never remarried after Mom died."

He picked up his mug. "I was a lot older than you are. And I wasn't alone. I had a wonderful daughter to love."

"I'm not alone, either. I have a wonderful father."

"Thank you for that." He lifted his mug in salute. "But it's not enough. And if you're honest with yourself, you'll admit that."

Lindsey took a sip of her cooling tea, the liquid as tepid as her heart had been until Nate had walked back into her life and awakened all sorts of dormant—and troublesome—emotions.

"I do get lonely sometimes." No harm admitting that much. "And I still miss Mark every single day." Especially when she awakened in the predawn hours and recalled how he used to pull her close in a warm, sleepy embrace for a few minutes before he left for an early shift. She'd always hated how his side of the bed cooled after he left.

Now it was always cold. And empty.

Like her heart.

"That's natural, honey. But so is wanting to have someone to love."

She set her mug down and pushed it aside. "Even if I was interested in Nate—and I'm not saying I am—he's a combat reporter, Dad. That's a high-risk profession."

"Doesn't mean he'll always be in a war zone."

"Maybe not. But from what he's told me, he's been in a lot of other dangerous places, too." She folded her hands on the table. "No, thanks. Been there, done that."

"Life is all about risk, Lindy. You can't let fear get in the way of living. Matter of fact, as I recall, you used to preach that to Nate. 'Take a chance, or be scaredy-pants.' That's what you used to tell him."

Lindsey furrowed her brow. "Did I really say that?"

"Yep. Has a catchy ring. I guess that's why it stuck with me."

She shrugged. "I've learned a thing or two since then. It's more prudent to be cautious."

"No arguments there. Not since this broken hip cramped my style." He drained his mug and pushed himself to his feet, using the table for leverage. "But I haven't given up gardening. I'm just a little more careful about where I step. Same's true with love. And now I'm done playing Dr. Phil for the day." He gestured to her empty mug. "Want some more tea?"

"I'm finished, thanks." When he reached for it, she touched his hand. "And thanks for the advice. I'll think about what you said."

"Good enough. And I'll keep praying. Join me if you want to." With a wink, he moved back to the sink.

She watched him, a rush of affection tightening her throat. He never gave up on his quest to help restore her faith. And thanks to his pushing and prodding, she was going to church more regularly now. Sending a few more prayers heavenward. Working harder to reestablish the once-strong link she'd felt with the Lord.

In the meantime, she was glad her dad was praying for her. Because with Nate shaking the foundations of the calm, placid life she'd established after returning to Starfish Bay, she could use all the help she could get.

Bingo.

Nate squinted at the screen of his laptop, felt for the glass of lemonade Lillian had offered after she'd agreed to let him plug into the modem in her office at the Orchid, and took a sip.

He should have started with the *Sacramento Bee* instead of wasting time Googling Mark Collier and wading through a bunch of unrelated pages. He'd hit pay dirt with the first blue headline on the *Bee's* archives page dated two and a half years earlier.

Mark Collier Memorial Fund Tops $350,000

That had to be Lindsey's husband. How many Mark Colliers would have lived in Sacramento? But why such a publicized memorial fund? Who was this guy, anyway?

He read the first two teaser lines of text below the date.

"Contributions to the memorial fund established in the name of Sacramento police officer Mark Collier..."

Lindsey's husband had been a police officer?

Not liking where this was heading, Nate clicked on the link to the full story and continued reading.

"...continue to arrive on an almost daily basis, according to a Police Department spokesperson, who predicted the total may exceed half a million dollars. At the direction of Mark's widow, who authorized the establishment of the fund, college grants will be given to area students who have demonstrated high academic abilities and an interest in pursuing a career in law enforcement.

"Collier was killed two years ago when he stepped in to break up an altercation between two youths in a parking garage and found himself in the middle of a drug deal. Off duty at the time, he suffered multiple stab wounds—including one to his aorta—and bled to death at the scene. His wife was also injured in the attack."

The sweet aftertaste of Lillian's lemonade soured in Nate's mouth.

Lindsey's husband hadn't just died, as she'd told him that first day at The Point.

He'd been murdered.

And she'd watched him die.

Nate closed his eyes and gripped the arms of the desk chair as the words he'd spewed out to her earlier replayed in his mind.

Do you know what it's like to lay there, too stunned to move, too stunned to help, and watch someone bleed to death an arm's reach away? Do you have any idea what it's like to feel that helpless?

Yeah, she did.

No wonder she'd looked shell-shocked at his tirade.

No wonder she carried a gun.

Sucking in a deep breath, he found himself turning to the God he'd distanced himself from for too long.

Lord, forgive me. Let her *forgive me.*

But truth be told, he didn't deserve forgiveness. He'd

hurt a grief-stricken widow who was still recovering from her own trauma. A woman who, despite the chaotic state of her world, had upended her life yet again to return home to assist her ailing father. To tutor struggling students. And now, to launch a crusade to save a place she—and others—loved.

More evidence of her strength.

Yet today, her emotional scars had gotten the upper hand. Because an experience like that affected you for the rest of your life. He knew.

But what of her physical scars? How badly had she been injured in the attack that had killed her husband?

Opening his eyes at last, Nate searched through the remaining stories about Lindsey's husband, looking for more information. But though he learned a lot more about Mark—he'd not only been a decorated police officer, but in his spare time he'd coached a boys' softball team in a troubled neighborhood and served on the board of Big Brothers—Nate found no more references to Lindsey's injuries.

"Did you get everything hooked up okay?"

At Lillian's question from behind him, Nate blinked. Took a breath. Tilted the screen of his laptop down. She'd offered to let him use her computer, but he'd wanted no record of his search anywhere except on his own machine. He didn't want the older woman to think he'd been prying into Lindsey's affairs.

Even if he had been.

Swiveling in the chair, he nodded. "Yes. No problem. In fact, I'm almost finished."

"That didn't take long." She cocked her head and gave him a once-over. "You know, you look a little peaked. Didn't the lemonade agree with you?"

"It was great." He picked up the half-empty cup to

take a sip, grasping it with both hands when he discovered his fingers were trembling. "I'll be out of your hair in a few minutes."

"Don't worry. I'm done for the night." She gave him another keen perusal. "Are you sure you're all right? Maybe you caught a chill out on The Point. I hope Lindsey's okay."

He shot her a puzzled look. "How did you know I was at The Point? With Lindsey?"

She chuckled. "Our mayor and her husband were driving our way on 101 for dinner and saw you and Lindsey start down the path back of the dental office. She told Genevieve. Word travels fast in Starfish Bay. You two keep stepping out together, gossip will have you paired up in no time. So a word to the wise—watch your p's and q's, unless there really is something going on between you two."

Although he tried to respond to Lillian's grin with a smile of his own, it was hard to fake good cheer. Much as he wished there *was* something going on between them, he had a sinking feeling the episode on The Point had dashed any chance of that as effectively as the sharp rocks at the base of the cliffs crushed the fragile shells carried by the waves.

"I'll keep that in mind. But I won't be around long, anyway."

"More's the pity. Genevieve thinks Lindsey's taken a fancy to you, and I have to say I agree. I also think the feeling is mutual."

He pivoted back toward his laptop, hoping the heat on his neck stayed below his collar. "And I think you two are jumping to too many wrong conclusions."

"Your pink ears tell a different story. But don't you worry, young man. Genevieve and I aren't ones to spread rumors. Our lips are sealed. We do wish you luck, though. And now I'll leave you to finish up."

The door clicked shut as the older woman departed, and he once more lifted the screen of his laptop, then powered down. He'd found the information he'd been after.

Now he had to find a way to make amends.

The fate of The Point wasn't looking rosy.

From her seat at the table in front of the room, Lindsey surveyed the town hall. Every chair had been claimed, and people were standing three deep around the perimeter. She'd been watching the faces as Louis Mattson made his presentation, and hostility had given way to receptiveness on many as he walked them through not only a preliminary design for Inn at the Point, but several examples of how Mattson Properties had integrated boutique hotels into other natural landscapes. He'd now moved on to a discussion of his very favorable projected economic impact on Starfish Bay.

She doodled on her notepad as he talked, anxious for them to get to the Q&A session. During his presentation, she'd jotted down a number of questions to supplement the ones she'd put together over the past few days. If none of the residents asked them, she intended to jump in.

"Well, that wraps up our formal remarks." Louis Mattson took in the town council and the residents with a sweeping smile. Tall and slender, his silver hair set off by his perfectly tailored dark gray suit, the man reeked class and integrity. This wasn't some sleazy operation that would make promises it never intended to keep. The company's record was stellar, based on Lindsey's research. It had won both architectural and environmental awards. There was no question in her mind that the proposed development for The Point would be tasteful.

But that still didn't mean it was the right thing to do.

"Thank you, Mr. Mattson." Susan adjusted her glasses and motioned toward the microphone in the middle of the center aisle between the rows of seats. "We'll now open the meeting to questions. Please line up behind the microphone and state your name for the record."

A third of the audience rose. Or so it seemed to Lindsey. She glanced at the mayor. Susan was frowning.

Lindsey positioned her own sheet of questions in front of her and settled back.

It was going to be a long night.

Things had not gone in Lindsey's favor.

From his seat in the last row of the town hall, Nate watched her pinched face as Susan prepared to wrap up the meeting. During the hour Q&A session, Louis Mattson had handled himself with aplomb, deflecting hostility and antagonism with reasoned, persuasive and empathetic responses. Nate estimated he'd won over at least half of those who'd come to the meeting tonight in full opposition to the plan. Some would revert to their previous position after Mattson packed up his dog-and-pony show and went back to San Francisco, but the scale appeared to be tipping in favor of approval.

Susan rose. "Thank you all for coming. And special thanks to Mr. Mattson and his team for their excellent presentation. The motion for a citizen vote on this matter has passed, and we'll work out the details at our next regular meeting in two weeks. You are all welcome to attend that as well. This meeting is adjourned." She banged her gavel.

As the crowd began to mill about and the murmur of conversation swelled to a crescendo, he felt a tap on his shoulder.

"I thought I saw you over here." Jack Callahan smiled at him as the crowd began to disperse. "You didn't say anything about attending when we chatted at the Mercantile today. And Lindsey didn't mention it, either."

"It was a spur-of-the-moment decision." Not that Lindsey would have known even if it hadn't been. Since their traumatic parting at The Point six days ago, she'd gone out of her way to avoid him. He always saw her for a couple of minutes when he showed up at the store to work with Jarrod, but her handoffs were quick and cool. And by the time he finished with the boy, she was always gone, leaving Jack in charge. He'd taken to dropping by at odd hours, hoping to catch her, but if she'd been there, she'd spotted him through the picture window by the counter and ducked out. Nor had he run into her at The Point, though he'd made several trips out there, too.

No one should be able to be that elusive in a town the size of Starfish Bay.

"I think the tide may have turned tonight."

At Jack's comment, Nate pulled himself back to the conversation. "You may be right."

"Lindsey's not going to be happy." He checked on his daughter, still at the front of the room, surrounded by a crowd of allies.

"Yeah. I know."

"She's been on the phone all week, trying to rally support. I heard talk of a letter-writing campaign, too.

And she called the papers in Eureka and Crescent City about tonight's meeting, but I don't think she had much luck interesting them in the affairs of our little community. As far as I could tell, there weren't any reporters here."

"I'm not surprised. A town council meeting is boring stuff for most newspapers. And this story isn't all that newsworthy in the big scheme of things."

It had great feature potential, though, with the kind of hook guaranteed to engage readers—a classic David and Goliath story. But maybe you had to have journalism or PR skills to know how to work that angle.

The kind he had.

A pang of guilt ricocheted through him.

"That's a fact. The Point doesn't matter to anyone but us." Jack sighed. "Guess I'll go on home. Looks like Lindsey will be here for a while."

Nate followed the direction of the older man's gaze. She was still surrounded by a crowd, her expression animated, her posture energized.

"You heading out, too?" Jack retrieved his jacket from the back of the chair in front of him, where he'd draped it during their conversation.

"I think I'll hang around a few more minutes."

"Okay. See you at the store." Lifting his hand, the man wove toward the exit.

Nate slipped into the shadows at the back of the town hall. Small clusters of people continued to congregate around the room, but slowly they all began to thin until at last Lindsey remained alone behind the head table.

Only then did her shoulders droop.

And that posture of defeat propelled him forward.

Intent on gathering up her purse and notepapers, she didn't see him approaching until he was mere feet away. Once she spotted him, she grasped the edge of the table and froze.

"Hi." He gave her a smile.

She didn't return it. "What are you doing here? I thought this wasn't your fight."

He deserved that. "I had a free evening."

"Well, I hope you were entertained." She dug around in her purse for her car keys.

"Lindsey…" He waited for her to look up. "I'm sorry about what happened at The Point the other day. I never meant to upset you."

She gave a stiff shrug and slung her purse over her shoulder. "I got over it."

"I doubt that. Now that I know what prompted it."

He heard her sharp intake of breath. "What are you talking about?"

"I'm a reporter. I know how to do research. It didn't take me long to find the stories about your husband in the *Bee's* archives." He gentled his voice. "I'm so sorry."

Bright spots of color appeared on her cheeks, and her fingers clenched around the strap of her purse, blanching her knuckles. "You could have asked instead of sneaking around behind my back."

"You've been difficult to pin down since that day. The minute I get to the Mercantile, you disappear."

She ignored that comment. "I don't know why you bothered, anyway."

"I think you do."

She ignored that, too. "I need to get home. It's late."

"Would you consider going somewhere with me for a cup of coffee? I'd like to talk with you."

"What's the point? We've been fighting ever since you came back, and in a handful of days you'll be gone.

I don't see any reason to invest any more effort in this relationship."

"I do. We had some great times together as kids. There's no reason we couldn't have some great times together as adults."

She responded with an impatient shake of her head. "Times change. People change. You can't live in the past."

"Aren't you doing that very thing?"

She blinked. "What do you mean?"

"You admitted you were scared after I suggested there might be more in store for us than friendship. Your fear must be coming from your experience with your husband. Isn't that holding on to the past, too?"

"No. That's being sensible. And I never said I was scared. Just…nervous." The lights in the room flicked on and off, a not-so-subtle message to clear out. She picked up her notebook and file folders. "Good night, Nate."

"Can I walk you to your car?"

"I'm in the back." With that, she swung away from him, aiming for an exit behind the table that separated them.

Once she pushed through the door, Nate shoved his hands in his pockets and made his way toward the door at the other end of the building, his fingers encountering his prized agate. His version of worry beads. Always, when he touched that small stone, he felt calmer. Soothed. Able to think more clearly.

Lindsey had rebuffed his olive branch tonight. But that didn't mitigate his need to make amends for the can of worms he'd opened on The Point. He needed to convince her the magic he recalled from their childhood friendship was still there. That he was coming to care for her as much now as he had then.

As he stood in the back of the now-quiet town hall where the fate of a local landmark hung in the balance, he could think of only one gesture that might penetrate the barrier she'd erected around her heart to keep him out.

But did he have the courage to take such a dramatic leap out of his comfort zone?

Chapter Nine

A cloud of dust rose as Lindsey flipped open the lid of a cardboard packing box. She paused long enough to sneeze twice, perusing the attic as she did so. The last time she'd ascended the pull-down stairs had been a few weeks before her marriage, when she'd come up in search of the small wedding photo of her mother she'd remembered seeing as a child. She'd wanted it to be the "something old" she carried as a bride.

That quest had been successful.

But she was having less success finding old photos of Starfish Bay Chapel.

As she plunged into the box, she hoped the others who'd volunteered to assist with the "Save the Point" campaign were having better luck. Using photos to help illustrate what an important role the headland and chapel had played in the lives of so many residents could be an effective strategy to stem the shifting tide of public sentiment on the issue. But unless she found a shot or two in this box, it didn't appear as if she was going to be able to contribute any photos to the effort.

At least she'd offered the front window of the Mercantile as a display space. Everyone in Starfish Bay came in once or twice a week, and she intended to post the photos and the accompanying written memories near the door.

Spotting an old photo album wedged into one side of the box, she took it in a firm grip and tugged it out. The rest of the contents slid into the cavity, and she huffed out a breath. Fitting the bulky album back in was going to take some effort. Worth it, though, if she found a photo or two.

Book in hand, she sat on one of the sheets of plywood her dad had laid on the rafters years ago and began to go through it.

The first few pages didn't yield any photos suitable for the campaign, but they did summon up a treasure trove of memories. There she was at seven or eight, clutching a spelling award, her dad and mom standing proudly behind her. Another showed her in a tutu, before or after some dance recital. In a Christmas photo, she and her mom sat cuddled under their ornament-bedecked tree, an array of gift-wrapped packages around them as Lindsey offered a gap-toothed grin to the camera.

A melancholy smile tugging at her lips, she turned the page.

Her smile faded.

In the center was a shot of her and Nathaniel on The Point, the corner of Starfish Bay Chapel visible in the background.

Had she found this photo a month ago, she had a feeling she'd have passed over it without anything more than a fleeting, "I wonder who that kid was?" or perhaps a vague memory of a long-ago friend. But she didn't have to wonder now. Their ages were about right for the time he'd lived in Starfish Bay. And the location was a dead giveaway. They were sitting on the bench at The Point.

She traced the edge of the slightly faded photo with one finger. Given the huge ice cream cones in their hands and the grins on their faces, it wasn't hard to figure out this had been taken in August, at the church's annual ice cream social. And from their joyful expressions, it had been an all's-right-with-the-world moment.

But that moment had also been fleeting, she suddenly recalled, as another memory tickled her brain. Seconds after this shot had been taken, she'd dropped her cone. It had landed with a splat at her feet, pointy end up. She'd been crushed.

And then Nathaniel had offered her his.

In the end, her dad had rounded up another cone for her and Nathaniel had kept his. Yet even as a kid, she'd been touched by his generosity. Just days before he'd told her how much he was looking forward to the social—and the free ice cream—since they didn't have a lot of treats like that at his house.

Proving again that selfishness wasn't part of Nate Garrison's character.

Then or now.

Stifling the niggle of regret that tugged at her conscience, she removed the photo and turned the page, searching for other pictures of the chapel. She had more important things to do than reminisce—or nurse regrets about ill-spoken comments.

Less than two minutes later, after scanning every picture on every page, she reached the end without finding any more shots of Starfish Bay Chapel. She hoped some of the other residents were having better luck.

After setting the photo of her and Nate on a carton

beside her, she rose to her knees and dug through the box, trying to eke out room for the album among the jumbled detritus of the past. Her fingers encountered a smooth round object blocking the way, and she pulled it out, balancing it in one hand as she slid the collection of photos back in with the other. Then she examined the small snow globe of an angel hovering over the stable in Bethlehem.

Yet another memory surfaced.

It was the Christmas Eve service, four months after the ice cream social. She'd noticed Nathaniel across the aisle, but she'd been too excited about the gifts waiting at home to pay much attention to him.

As they'd all been leaving, though, he'd managed to work his way over to her through the crowd. He'd only had time to thrust a small wrapped package into her hands and murmur "thank you" before his mother had hurried him back toward their car—and out of her life—under the dark, starless sky.

She hadn't seen him again until he'd walked into the Mercantile twenty-five years later, all grown up.

Lindsey sat back on her heels, cradling the globe in her hands. In the bounty of Christmas that had always characterized her childhood, somehow this small offering had been misplaced. And eventually forgotten.

She took another look at the photo of the two of them, balanced on the carton beside her.

Once more, guilt began to gnaw at her.

Nate had come back to Starfish Bay because of the happy memories he harbored of his brief stay here. Some of those memories included her. Yet she'd rebuffed every attempt he'd made to rekindle their friendship.

And she knew why.

Fear.

Just as Nate had pointed out yesterday.

Though she'd countered by saying she was nervous, his assessment had been accurate. She was scared. For a very simple reason. The feelings he awakened in her threatened to disrupt the quiet, safe little world she'd retreated to after Mark's death. She might have told everyone her father's accident had brought her home, but in all honesty, she'd been glad to have an excuse to come back to the sheltering shores of Starfish Bay. Here, she'd hoped to heal. And find answers.

She suspected those were the same reasons Nate had returned. That he, too, considered this place a haven. Perhaps from the traumatic battlefield experience he'd mentioned. Or from whatever culpability he felt over the death of his mother. Hadn't he told her it was his own fault he'd lost her and ended up in foster care?

While she hadn't pushed him to share any of the details of those experiences, Lindsey was curious about his past. Why was he afraid to let people get close? What had he meant when he'd told her once he didn't need her to lay more guilt on him because he had plenty already? What drove him to fling himself into the line of fire in his work, no matter the personal risk?

She hadn't exactly laid the groundwork for such confidences, though. Nor did she want him to think she was ready—or willing—to take their relationship to a different level. But they'd been friends once. Good friends, based on the evidence she was unearthing and the memories that were surfacing. The least she could do after his long journey was let him know she was willing to be his friend again.

Given their tumultuous reunion to date, however,

figuring out a way to do that could turn out to be a bigger challenge than saving The Point.

"So are you leaving this weekend?"

At Jarrod's question, Nate looked up from the document they'd been reading on his computer in the Mercantile's coffee nook.

"When do you start school?"

"Not for almost two weeks."

"Then I'm staying at least another week." It was a spur-of-the-moment decision, but it felt right. He'd taken six weeks off, and he was only approaching the halfway mark. Returning to Chicago early held no appeal, and he had nowhere else to go.

The boy's face lit up. "Seriously?"

"Seriously. We're not done with our article yet."

"Cool."

His phone began to vibrate, and he pulled it off his belt to check caller ID. As his editor's name flashed on the display, he frowned. Clark was an email junkie, reverting to the phone only when he had a very serious matter to discuss.

Nate's pulse kicked up a notch.

"Check out that last paragraph again and see if there's anything else I might be able to use, okay?" He rose and started toward the front door.

"Yeah. Sure."

Once he was in the parking lot, he tapped the talk button. "Hi, Clark."

"Nate. Got your piece on Starfish Bay. You've been holding out on me."

The fried egg he'd eaten at the Orchid for breakfast congealed in his stomach. "That must mean you plan to run it."

"I don't *plan* to; I already did. Jeff Gorski is on vacation and we've been using syndicated columnists to fill his Viewpoint spot. Your piece will run in tomorrow's edition. It's online now."

The whole world was already reading his private thoughts? He fought down a surge of panic.

"So what else do you have along these lines?"

"Nothing. It was a one-time shot, Clark."

"There must be more where that came from."

"Touchy-feely stuff isn't my shtick."

"You could have fooled me. Look, I know you like the action assignments. I get that. But there's no reason you can't do both. I think you're on to something. We're already getting hits on this from our syndication partners. Especially from West Coast papers."

"That's great." He tried to muster some enthusiasm. Lindsey would be happy, even if he was unnerved. "But I don't know what else I'd write about."

"Personal experiences. And you've had plenty of those. I bet you've got another idea already noodling around in your brain."

Nate thought of the piece Jarrod was helping him research. Could he work that into a commentary rather than a straight reporting article?

"Your silence tells me you do."

"No." Nate jumped back into the conversation. "Maybe. I don't know." He massaged his temples and looked toward The Point, hidden behind the dense forest, but waiting if he needed it. "I have to think about this."

"You do that. In the meantime, we'll see what kind of reader reaction we get to this first foray. You still coming back in three weeks?"

"That's the plan."

"Good. I've got a couple of assignments in mind for you."

"Overseas?"

"No. I'll keep you in the States for a while, unless you're ready to go back to the Middle East."

"Not yet." Maybe never.

"Okay. I'll be in touch in a day or two with some feedback. Nice work."

"Thanks."

As his boss signed off, Nate slipped the phone back onto his belt, willed the mutiny in his stomach to subside, and rejoined Jarrod. Ten minutes later, after Cindy reclaimed her son and disappeared into the aisles of the store to do a little shopping, he checked out his piece in the online edition of the *Tribune*.

Seeing it in print restarted the churning in his gut.

The copy desk had added a headline: "A Tribute to Touchstones." They'd also run his file photo, a shot taken a year or so ago while he was on assignment in Afghanistan. He'd forgotten they used author photos in commentary pieces. Seeing his words in print was bad enough. The picture made him feel doubly exposed.

"Everything go okay with Jarrod?"

At Lindsey's question, he looked up over the screen on his laptop. She hadn't said much to him since their encounter at the town council meeting two days ago, but a subtle nuance in her demeanor gave him hope that for some reason that was about to change.

"Yes. He's doing well."

Before he could motion her over and show her the piece on his screen, she pulled her hands from behind her back, where they'd been clasped, and held up a small snow globe.

"I was going through some boxes in the attic, hoping

to find some photos to add to our collection——" she gestured toward the front window, where pictures and reminiscences of The Point and the chapel had been appearing over the past twenty-four hours "——and found this. Do you remember it?"

He stared at the small globe. Of course he remembered it. He'd emptied his coin bank to buy it, then labored over his selection while on a shopping trip with his mother. He'd wanted to buy a special Christmas present for Lindsey to thank her for being his friend.

In the end, though, it had turned out to be a farewell present.

He couldn't believe she still had it.

"Yeah. I do." The words came out ragged, and he cleared his throat.

Cradling the globe as if it was from Tiffany's instead of a five-and-dime in Crescent City, she moved closer. "To be honest, I'd forgotten about it. But once I pulled it out, I remembered you giving it to me the last time I saw you. As a matter of fact, I've been remembering a lot about the time we spent together. And the fun we had. And your kindness."

She reached into the pocket of her shirt and pulled out a small photo, laying it on the table beside him. "I found this, too. I'd like to post it in the memory display. Along with this. If you're okay with it." She added a small typed slip of paper.

The photo, too, brought back a rush of memories, so vivid he could almost taste the double chocolate mint ice cream he'd consumed that day. He scanned her write-up.

Nate Garrison and Lindsey Callahan Collier, Starfish Bay Chapel ice cream social. Memories like this last forever—and call people home.

She'd added the year at the bottom.

A rush of warmth flowed through him, and his throat tightened again. "Yeah, I'm okay with it."

Still cradling the globe in one hand, she picked up the photo and paper with the other and slipped them back into her pocket. "Look, I'm sorry I said you were selfish that day at The Point. You've never been selfish."

Some of the warmth evaporated. "Yeah, I have been." His father had drilled that into him.

"I don't believe that."

"Believe it." Maybe someday he'd tell her about that painful episode from his past. But this wasn't that day, despite her public gesture of friendship with the photo. "I did do one unselfish thing recently, though. Take a look." He angled the computer and motioned her to come closer.

She hesitated for a second, then circled the table and leaned down toward the screen. Her lips parted as she began to read, and she twisted her head to stare at him. "I don't understand."

"I sent the piece to my editor. He liked it. It'll run tomorrow in the spot usually reserved for one of our regular columnists, who's on vacation. The online edition comes out earlier."

"No." She shook her head, twin furrows creasing her brow. "I understand that you decided to send the piece in. What I meant was, why did you change your mind?"

With her face inches from his, he found himself mesmerized by the flecks of gold in her brown irises. By the long lashes framing her eyes. By the soft, supple shape of her lips.

Willing his pulse to steady, he shifted his focus back to the screen. "After I cooled down the other day, I thought about what you said. And I agreed. A piece like this might help create some positive public sentiment about The Point. And it's already been picked up for syndication. From some papers in this part of the country, in fact."

She didn't respond at once, and when the silence lengthened he risked a glance at her—only to have his lungs short-circuit at the tenderness in her eyes.

"This was a huge stretch for you, wasn't it?"

Breathe, Garrison.

"It's a lot different than the stuff I cover on my regular beat." He knew she was looking for more than that, but he didn't trust his voice.

To his surprise, she didn't push. Instead, she laid a gentle hand on his shoulder. "Thank you."

"Don't thank me until we see if it has any effect."

"It's already had an effect."

She wasn't talking about the Save the Point campaign. Her soft, personal tone told him that. And he didn't pretend to misunderstand.

"I'm glad."

She gave him a tentative smile. Removed her hand from his shoulder. Moistened her lips and straightened up, her fingers still wrapped around the snow globe. "I don't know how much sightseeing you've managed to work in since you've been here, but I was thinking about going hiking in Prairie Creek State Park tomorrow morning. Would you like to join me?"

"Are you going to the redwoods?"

At Jarrod's question, Lindsey swung toward the boy as he rounded a shelving unit, a bag of pretzels in his hand. "I don't know. We're, uh, talking about it and, uh..."

"Yes," Nate replied, answering both their questions.

"Cool! Could I come, too?"

Lindsey pivoted back to Nate. She seemed to be trying to communicate some message, but he didn't have a clue what it was. So he, too, stalled.

"We'd have to talk to your mother first."

"Okay. I'll get her." The boy took off.

The instant he was out of earshot, Nate gestured Lindsey closer and lowered his voice. "What's going on? I got your vibes but not your message. And talk fast. My guess is he'll be back in less than sixty seconds."

Following his prompt, she leaned down. "Cindy told me he used to love to go to the redwoods with his dad. But since he died, Jarrod has refused every offer she's made to take him back. I think this might be a breakthrough of some sort. Although to be honest," she caught her lower lip between her teeth and swept a few imaginary crumbs from the table with her fingers, "I wasn't planning on a threesome."

She'd been hoping this would be more like a date.

That was the best piece of news he'd had all day. No, all year.

But it wasn't going to happen tomorrow.

"I'd prefer it just be the two of us, too. Based on what you've told me, though, I don't see how we can say no."

She sighed. "Me, neither. I guess we'll—"

"Here's my mom." Jarrod rejoined them, tugging Cindy along by the hand behind him.

"What's this I hear about a trip to the redwoods?" She addressed the question to both of them, her expression equal parts hope and caution.

"I already told you, Mom." Jarrod heaved a sigh. "They're going to the redwoods tomorrow to hike. Can I go with them? Please?"

"Were you invited?"

The boy gave her a blank look. Then a faint flush crept across his cheeks. "I can't remember. I think so."

Nate stepped in. "We'd be happy to have him join us."

"Are you sure?" Cindy addressed the question to Lindsey, her expression skeptical.

"Absolutely. I haven't been for a while, and I don't remember all the best trails. I bet Jarrod would be a great guide."

"I would! I could take you on the Brown Creek trail. We might even see some banana slugs."

"Banana slugs? Sold." Nate grinned at him.

As Cindy regarded her son's animated face, Nate detected a slight shift in her features. A subtle easing of tension, perhaps. "If you're sure, that would be fine."

At Jarrod's whoop of joy, two customers poked their heads around the ends of aisles to check out the activity in the coffee nook.

Cindy shushed him, discussed arrangements with Lindsey and paid her bill, then led a smiling Jarrod out of the store.

As the door closed behind them with a cheery ring of the bell, Lindsey rejoined Nate, still holding the snow globe. "Thanks for doing that."

"Not a problem. It would be nice to go back to Chicago knowing my trip accomplished some good."

"Maybe a lot of good." She indicated the computer. "My guess is that piece will resonate with a lot of people. It could end up saving The Point."

"I think you're expecting too much from one article."

"I've read it. I'm not expecting too much."

He smiled at her. "You're very good for my ego."

"I wasn't so good the other day at The Point when I

said you were selfish. And everything that's happened since has proven how wrong I was. This." She hefted the snow globe. "That." She pointed to the computer, where the touchstones story remained on the screen. "Your volunteer tutoring with Jarrod. And what you did for him just now."

"What I did just now was the result of a prod from my conscience. I'd have preferred to have the day alone with you."

"But you did it, anyway."

He shrugged off her praise. "A moment of weakness. But I'd still like to have some alone time with you. Maybe we can plan another outing?"

The small bell beside the cash register summoned her, and she backed away. "Let's see how tomorrow goes, okay?"

"Sure."

Yet as he watched her disappear around the shelving and settled back in his chair, he didn't have to wonder how tomorrow was going to go.

Because if that was his ticket to a real date with Lindsey, he intended to do everything in his power to ensure it went very, very well.

Chapter Ten

One hundred and two messages.

Nate's eyes widened as he logged into his work email and saw the tally since yesterday. What the…?

He clicked the inbox and scanned the names. Almost all unfamiliar. But a quick sweep of the subject lines gave him his answer.

All the emails were reader responses to his touchstones piece.

Wow.

Never, in his entire career, had he gotten more than a dozen emails about any single article. Even that many were rare.

He leaned sideways in his chair in the coffee nook to check on Lindsey, whose back was to him as she talked with her father behind the counter. Reading email had simply been a time killer while they waited for Jarrod, but he'd never expected such an overwhelming response. Wait until she saw this.

As he began opening the messages, he was taken aback by the outpouring of support and gratitude expressed by the readers.

Lindsey had been right. The piece had resonated with a lot of people.

While he read the heartfelt letters, his phone began to vibrate. He pulled it off and stood, greeting his editor on the way to the door.

The man didn't bother with niceties. "How many emails have you gotten?"

"More than a hundred." He pushed through the door.

"We've gotten dozens, here, too. I figured you'd been buried. And the piece hasn't even run in syndication yet. You think any more about the talk we had?"

"Not a lot."

"Make it a priority. You've been hiding your talent under a bushel basket."

"I thought you liked my investigative and war coverage?"

"I do. But this piece sings. Sorry to get poetic on you, but that sums it up. You need to think about doing more of this."

An older model Toyota pulled into the parking lot, Ruth Watson at the wheel. He'd exchanged a few words with the cheery, red-haired young mother on occasion when she'd dropped Jarrod off for his tutoring sessions, and he raised a hand in response to her wave.

The youngster in question hung out the window and flapped his hand, his face alight with excitement.

"I'll do that." He grinned and waved back. "But right now I have an important engagement."

"I want you to promise me you'll work on another piece along these lines."

As Jarrod climbed out of the car filled with the Watson kids, Nate thought again of the article on children who'd lost parents. "I do have a subject in mind for one more piece."

"Perfect. When can you have it ready?"

"A week, maybe. But won't Gorski's column be running again by then?"

"We'll find a place for yours. You enjoying yourself out there?"

"It's been a good visit."

"Not too good, I hope. We want you back, Nate."

"I'm counting on that." Of course he was going back. He'd never considered doing otherwise. Though truth be told, the thought of returning to the Windy City was becoming less and less appealing.

"All right. Hold that thought. And get working on that column." The line went dead.

"Hi, Mr. Garrison." Jarrod trotted over to join him as he slid his phone back onto his belt. "You ready for the hike?"

"All set."

Ruth rolled down her window. "Cindy said you'd be back around two. I tucked my cell number in Jarrod's pocket. Give me a call when you're close and I'll swing back by here and pick him up."

"You want us to drop him off at your house?"

The woman grinned. "I have no idea where I'll be at that point, but home isn't on the list. We have an orthodontist visit, swimming lessons, story hour at the library—it's probably safer if you call."

"Got it." Nate smiled back. "Have fun."

Rolling her eyes, she waved, put the car in gear and took off down 101.

Jarrod was already halfway to the door of the Mercantile, and he called over his shoulder. "Is Ms. Collier ready?"

"Let's check."

But he already knew the answer. She'd keep her

promise and go through with this outing, but she wasn't ready. The minute he'd arrived this morning he'd sensed her nervousness. And second thoughts.

And he knew why she felt that way.

Like him, she was falling more and more under the spell of their reawakening friendship. Remembering all the happy times—and discovering that despite the passage of time, despite the trauma they'd both endured, despite experiences that had left them both wary, whatever chemistry had attracted them to each other as children was just as strong as it had been twenty-five years ago.

Maybe stronger.

As he stepped inside and found Lindsey engaged in conversation with Jarrod, a smile tugging at her lips in response to the boy's enthusiasm, he modified that. No maybes about it. The attraction was a lot stronger.

What that meant for their future, he didn't know. But as her gaze connected with his and a becoming flush rose on her cheeks, he resolved to find out ASAP.

"I think he's enjoying himself." Lindsey reached for another oatmeal cookie from the bag atop her small daypack, then settled in against the downed redwood she and Nate were using for a backrest. Jarrod appeared to be fighting some imaginary battle in the small clearing where they'd decided to take a break, brandishing a stick as a sword while darting back and forth between the hollowed-out base of a living redwood and the giant ferns that gave the place a prehistoric feel.

"That makes two of us."

She transferred her attention to Nate—and her heart skipped a beat.

Man, he looked fabulous today.

Worn jeans molded his lean hips, and his snug black T-shirt revealed some impressive biceps and pecs. The man might be in a so-called sedentary occupation, but it was obvious his assignments kept him anything but deskbound. He looked more than capable of going head-to-head with the special-forces soldiers he must have encountered in the Middle East. Add a chiseled chin and those amazing blue eyes—it was a killer package.

A sudden wave of guilt blindsided her, and she forced herself to turn back toward Jarrod. "I can't tell you how grateful Cindy was for our willingness to bring Jarrod along. She thinks he might finally be…"

"Lindsey."

Her voice stuttered at Nate's quiet but firm tone. And when his hand came to rest on her shoulder, when the warmth of his fingers seeped through the thin cotton of her own T-shirt, her lungs shorted out.

The bite of cookie she'd just taken got stuck halfway down her throat, and she groped for her bottle of water. Twisted the cap. Took a long gulp.

Only then did she venture a look at her companion.

He hadn't moved, except for the hand he'd dropped to her shoulder. His long legs, crossed at the ankle, were still stretched in front of him. His other hand remained clasped around the bottle of water propped on the needle-covered ground beside him.

"We need to talk."

"About what?" Her words came out in a croak.

"Us."

The man didn't beat around the bush.

But he was right. Hadn't she asked him on this outing to find out more about his background? To open the door to friendship?

Except she was getting cold feet. Make that frigid

feet. Because opening the door to friendship could also open the door to more.

Take a chance, or be scaredy-pants.

Her old admonition to the man beside her echoed in her mind. Her dad's advice had been sound. She shouldn't let fear get in the way of living. Mark would be the first one to tell her that. Her husband had lived every minute of his life, never letting worry or fear rob one minute of joy from his days.

You can do this, Lindsey. Take it one step at a time. You're not making any commitments here. You're just... keeping your options open. Exploring the possibilities. You don't have to feel guilty about it.

The cookie snapped in half in her fingers, and she set it carefully on her lap. "Okay."

He seemed taken aback by her acquiescence. "Okay?"

"Yeah. Okay." She brushed the crumbs off her unsteady fingers. "I guess we do need to talk."

"I didn't think it would be this easy."

She leveled a direct look at him. "It won't be. We had a great relationship as kids, from everything I've been remembering, but even though I still feel a certain... chemistry...between us, life's a lot more complicated now."

"Life's always been complicated. For me, anyway." Bleakness dulled the color of his eyes to the hue of the sea before a storm.

Her throat contracted, reminding her she wasn't the only one with fears and baggage. "I'm beginning to realize that. I had no idea your home life as a child was so difficult."

He lifted one shoulder. "You lived in a perfect world. One where the kinds of things that went on in my house weren't even on the radar screen. I envied you that, you know. And prayed my own family could become more like yours. For a while, I thought those prayers had been answered."

"Until your father started drinking again?"

"Yeah." He picked up his water and took a swig.

"What happened after you left here?" She chose her next words with care. "You implied once it was your own fault you lost your mom and ended up in foster care. But I don't believe that."

"My dad did."

She could tell he was trying for a dispassionate tone, but she heard the bitterness—and hurt—underneath. She touched his hand. "What happened?"

For several seconds, he regarded her fingers resting against his sun-browned skin. "I've never talked about this. With anyone."

And he wasn't going to begin with her. She got the message.

Quashing her disappointment, she started to retract her hand. "I understand. I didn't mean to…"

He grabbed for her fingers, twining them with his, and locked onto her eyes. "But I'll make an exception for you."

The significance of his comment—and its implications—were clear. But scary as that was, it also warmed a place deep in her heart that had long lain cold and dormant.

Without relinquishing her hand, he lifted his gaze toward the sunbeams filtering through the giant trees and drew up one knee. "I'll try to give you the condensed version. After we left Starfish Bay, Mom and I moved to Ohio, where she'd grown up. Dad followed us, still hoping to patch things up. I don't know, he might have convinced her eventually. He did stop drinking again for a while, and he could be very persuasive. And I know they loved each other. But he never got the chance."

She waited in silence while he took another long swallow of water.

"One Saturday morning, the spring after we left here, Mom woke up with a bad headache. For the first time in my life, I was attending a real school instead of being homeschooled, and that was the day of the annual picnic. I'd made a couple of friends, and we'd planned to meet there and hang out. Mom said she didn't feel well enough to take me, and I was furious. So I called one of my buddies, and his mother agreed to pick me up."

Nate's voice flattened as if he was trying to distance himself from the telling. "By the time I left, Mom's headache was worse and she seemed a little off balance. I asked her to call the doctor, but she'd ended up with a nasty staph infection after giving birth to me and avoided doctors and hospitals after that. She said she'd take some aspirin and that I shouldn't worry. But I worried anyway. I had bad vibes about the whole thing. So a couple of hours later, I told the other kid's mother I didn't feel well, and she drove me home."

Lindsey heard the sound of plastic puckering as his fingers crushed the water bottle.

"I found Mom on the floor in the kitchen. She'd died from a cerebral hemorrhage. My dad took me in, but he blamed me for her death. He said I was selfish. That I should have stayed with her if she was sick, or at least called him. He started drinking again, too. And disappearing for days at a stretch. Child Protective Services finally took me away, after someone reported the neglect. He died a year later in a one-car, drunk-driving accident."

As Nate ended his story, Lindsey felt the pressure of tears in her throat. All these years, he'd carried around a boatload of guilt. Believed he was responsible for his mother's death, and that his selfishness had killed any hope of a reconciliation that could have made them a real family again. And how must he have felt, knowing his father had been willing to try and stay sober in order to get his wife back—but keeping his son wasn't worth the same effort?

The answer was obvious.

Unworthy.

Lindsey closed her eyes, her heart aching for that lost, neglected little boy. And for the solitary man beside her, whose quest for—validation? forgiveness? redemption? all of the above?—had driven him cross country, back to the one place where life had made sense.

She tightened her grip on his fingers, which remained entwined with hers. "What happened to your mom wasn't your fault. You were just a little boy who wanted to go to a school picnic and sample the normal childhood that you'd missed out on for most of your life. Your father's blame was grossly misplaced."

"I'd like to believe that. But the truth is, even though I was a kid, I knew whatever Mom had was more than a headache. I shouldn't have gone. Dad was right. About that, at least."

"And you've spent your life trying to atone for that mistake. To prove you're worthy." She studied his face. "That's why you put yourself in the line of fire, isn't it?"

He frowned at her. "I think you're getting way too

psychological. I needed to earn a living. I'm a decent writer, and I like action, so I put the two together and found a job that suits me. End of story."

"Is it?"

"Yeah. It's an interesting job. I like it."

"Then why did you take a leave of absence?"

A muscle twitched in his jaw. "You don't cut a guy any slack, do you? But then, you never did." The ghost of a smile softened his taut lips and took the edge off his words. "I don't recall little Lindsey Callahan ever backing away from a challenge. She was one spunky kid."

"I'm Lindsey Collier now. A different person." She played with the broken cookie in her lap. "It's funny, though. With you, I still feel like Lindsey Callahan."

"And you still make me feel like the Nathaniel I was for those few months in Starfish Bay. Before my mom died. Before foster care. Before Afghanistan."

The slight roughening of his voice on the last word was telling. "What happened there, Nate?"

"Too much." His answer came out flat. "Embedded combat coverage is brutal. You live with the troops. Eat with them. Listen to their fears and hopes and dreams. Become friends with them. And then you watch them die, one by one."

A shudder rippled through her. "I can't even imagine."

He gave a stiff shrug. "After a while, you learn to deal with it."

"How? Based on what you've said about your faith, I'm assuming you didn't turn to God for answers."

"No. Until I came back here, I hadn't spoken to God in years. I coped by shutting off the horror. Shoving it into a corner and not thinking about it. Except at night, in the darkness, when sleep wouldn't come and the images strobed across my mind. But for the most part, my technique worked. Until the day I went out with an advance squad on a reconnaissance mission."

He squeezed her fingers in a numbing grip, but she didn't flinch. Whatever was coming next, she knew it had been the catalyst for his cross-country trip to Starfish Bay.

"We were walking along a deserted road. The next thing I knew, the world exploded. A whole sequence of roadside bombs had detonated. I remember flying through the air, surrounded by screams and chaos. I landed on my back, four feet from the sergeant. A good guy. Brave. Smart. One semester away from his engineering degree. A wife back home. A baby on the way. He was facing me. His lips were moving, but there was no sound. And there was a huge hole in his chest."

Nate blinked. Sucked in a ragged breath. "I watched the sand underneath him turn dark as the life seeped out of him. I couldn't help him. I couldn't help any of them. All twelve of those soldiers died while I walked away with six stitches and a concussion. It didn't make sense. I should have died, too. They were all better men than me. They deserved to live. Why was I the only one who survived?"

His voice broke, and Lindsey caught the sheen in his eyes before he shifted away on the pretense of looking for the cap for the water bottle.

That last, tortured question, torn from his very soul, told her at last why he was here. He'd come back to the one place where the world had treated him kindly, hoping to find answers that would help him once more make sense of his life and give it purpose.

All at once, Lindsey saw her own trials in a new

light. Yes, she'd suffered trauma. But she had mostly happy memories. Plus a healthy amount of self-esteem. The only pleasant memories the man beside her had were confined to a few months in Starfish Bay. And the one man who could have shored up his son's self-esteem had instead left him with a legacy of guilt and shame.

It was tragic.

Yet despite the adversities he'd faced, despite any shortcomings he might see in himself, Nate Garrison had grown into a generous, caring man. One who deserved her affection and respect, if not more.

Shoving the daypack between them out of the way, Lindsey scooted closer and angled toward him. Hesitated. Then followed her heart and reached out to him.

He jerked as her fingers made contact with the slight stubble on his cheek. When he turned toward her, his lashes were spiky with moisture.

"I'm so sorry." She choked out the words, wishing she could offer more. Support. Sympathy. Solace. Something—anything—that would mitigate the pain this man had suffered. But she came up blank. "Even though I can't answer your question, I can tell you this. I'm glad you survived. Otherwise, our paths would never have crossed again."

He stroked his thumb over the back of her hand, loosening his grip as his eyes softened with gratitude...and another emotion she chose to ignore for the moment. "Thank you for saying that."

"It's true. Our reunion has had a few rough edges, but on the whole I think it's been a positive thing." As she spoke, she eased her hand from his and tried to unobtrusively flex her fingers to get the blood flowing again.

He homed in on her subtle gesture at once, twin creases denting his brow. "What's wrong with your hand?"

She tried to tuck it behind her, but he reached around and tugged it back into view, staring at the white ridges as he cradled it with his long, lean fingers. "Why didn't you tell me I was hurting you?"

"Your story was too compelling to interrupt. And I'm fine." She wiggled her fingers to demonstrate. Already they were beginning to take on a normal skin tone again. "See?"

"There's a faster way."

Before she could object, he began to massage her hand, his touch tender and caring.

Her protest died in her throat.

"Look what I found!"

A small, grimy hand suddenly appeared in front of her face, a bright yellow banana slug resting in the palm.

"That's a big one."

Nate's hoarse comment registered somewhere in her peripheral consciousness. As did the small creature in Jarrod's palm. But front and center was the unexpected feeling of contentment that swept over her as Nate continued to massage her fingers—and her heart.

"Hey, how come you guys are holding hands?"

It took a second for Jarrod's question to register. Once it did, she jerked her hand free.

This time Nate let her go.

As she scrambled to think of a way to explain the situation, Nate stepped in. "Because we're friends."

"Yeah?" Jarrod gave them a once-over. "That's cool."

"How about another cookie before we start back to

the trailhead?" Lindsey snatched up the bag, hoping to distract him.

"Okay. Let me put this little guy back where I found him. That's what my dad always said to do." His animation dimmed a notch. "We used to go to the redwoods sometimes, just him and me. For a little while today, it kind of felt like he was with me. Maybe I'll ask my mom to bring me back again soon."

Without waiting for a response, he scurried back toward the edge of the clearing.

"Touchstones." Lindsey looked over at Nate.

"Yeah. I had the same thought. Seems like we're in sync. In a lot of ways." He leaned closer and stroked his index finger down the back of her hand.

Lindsey was saved from having to respond by Jarrod's reappearance. But as she doled out the last of the cookies, she knew Nate was right. They were in sync.

As for what the future held, she had no idea.

But for the first time since Mark's death, she was looking forward to finding out.

Chapter Eleven

"My word." Genevieve stopped beside Nate's table in the Orchid Café and refilled his lemonade. "You've created quite a stir with that article of yours."

Lost in the memory of Lindsey's hand in his as they'd hiked back to the trailhead yesterday, Nate had to forcibly shift gears. It seemed everyone in town had read or heard about his piece since Lindsey had posted a copy—with his permission—at the Mercantile.

"I hope it helps."

"It already is. I can feel the mood swinging in our favor. And we're going to be getting even more publicity this week. A woman from one of the TV stations in San Francisco called early this morning. They're sending a crew up to do a feature for tomorrow night's program and needed two rooms for tonight. And a reporter from the *San Francisco Examiner* made a reservation, too."

Amazing. None of the battlefield stories he'd risked his life for had ever received this kind of attention, though they'd won a few writing awards. It had taken a subject that required him to risk his heart rather than his neck to truly touch people.

The *email full* message on his computer this morning was further proof of that.

Nate picked up his last French fry. "Any interest from the local media?"

"You bet. There was a woman from the Crescent City paper nosing around yesterday. And see that guy over there?" She gestured with the pitcher toward the stool-lined counter, the lemonade sloshing dangerously close to the rim. "He's with the *Eureka Times-Standard*. You want me to introduce you? You could give him an interview."

"No." His response was swift. And adamant. "I'm more comfortable on the other side of the pen."

"I can see why. That piece of yours brought a tear to my eye." She rested the pitcher on the edge of the table. "I have my own touchstone, you know. A special place back home in Georgia. I always stop by when Lillian and I head east for our annual visit."

Nate's email was full of stories like that. But he was curious about Genevieve's. "Tell me about it."

A wistful smile playing at her lips, she settled the pitcher on the table and stared into space. "It's an abandoned peach orchard on the edge of town. Been there for as long as I can remember. Doesn't mean a thing to anyone else. But every time I pass by, I think of the day my Sam proposed to me, with the wind rustling the leaves and the sky so blue and the smell of ripe peaches in the air. For that moment in time, everything was perfect."

Just like his months in Starfish Bay.

She sniffed. Blinked. Gave him a wavery smile as she picked up the pitcher. "Sorry. The waterworks turn on whenever I think of that place. The smell of fresh peaches can do it to me, too. Anyone watching me bake a peach pie would think I'd lost a screw or two. You want anything else this morning?"

"No, thanks. I've reached my limit."

"You put away a hearty lunch." She examined his clean plate. "Must still be making up for all the calories you expended on your hike yesterday."

He should have known someone would spot them in the redwoods and spread the word. "Don't tell me the mayor saw us at the park, too?"

"Not this time. Cindy and Jarrod stopped in for dinner last night. That boy was more talkative than he's been since before his father died, God rest his soul. I heard all about your outing—the banana slug, the oatmeal cookies, the giant ferns...the hand-holding." She gave him a knowing wink.

His neck warmed. "I was massaging her fingers."

Genevieve hooted, drawing the attention of several nearby diners. "Now that's a new one. I'll have to pass it on to Lillian. She'll get a kick out of it."

The reporter at the counter looked their way and narrowed his eyes. Like he was trying to figure out why he recognized Nate.

His cue to exit. Before the man connected him to the combat photo that had run with his touchstones piece.

He rose, keeping his back to the reporter. "Don't get your hopes up, Genevieve. I'm only a temporary resident in Starfish Bay."

"It's not my hopes that matter, young man. It's yours. And I'm praying you're smart enough to recognize a good thing when you see it."

With that, she bustled back toward the counter. Giving him no chance to respond.

And what would he have said, anyway? She was right. He did recognize a good thing when he saw it.

The question was, did Lindsey feel the same way? And if she did, how could they make this work? She'd left Starfish Bay once; he had a feeling she wasn't inclined to do so again. Yet his life was elsewhere.

Or it had been.

But maybe there were options.

Mulling that over, he pushed through the café door and looked toward The Point. That had always been a good place for thinking through problems. And talking to God. He'd done a lot of the latter once upon a time, under the guidance of Reverend Tobias.

Maybe it was time to give it another shot.

"What's this I hear about hand-holding in the redwoods?"

At her father's question, Lindsey jerked toward him and promptly dropped the box of tuna she'd retrieved from the back room to restock the shelves. Cans rolled in every direction. But instead of being aggravated, she was grateful for the excuse to get down on her hands and knees and hide the telltale flush she knew was turning her cheeks bright pink.

"That depends. What did you hear? And who did you hear it from?" She kept her face averted from the counter as she reached for one of the wayward cans.

"I heard it from Jarrod. He and Cindy stopped in this morning. And according to your young guide, Nate told him it was because you were friends."

Great. How was she supposed to refute an eyewitness account?

"Well, we are."

She braced for his response, but to her surprise he remained silent.

Lindsey used the reprieve to gather up the rest of the

cans and give her heightened color a chance to recede. By the time she stood, box of tuna in hand, she felt more composed.

Until she saw her father's speculative—and not altogether happy—expression.

"What's wrong?" She kept her distance, bracing the box against her chest.

"Nothing." He fiddled with the dome over the cookies, resetting it in the grooves around the edge of the plate. "Much."

At his tacked-on caveat, Lindsey tightened her grip on the box. "Okay, Dad. Let's have it. What's up?"

He looked around the store. They were alone, as he well knew. So why was he stalling? That wasn't Jack Callahan's style.

"I've been thinking about you and Nate." He paused. "You know he's leaving soon."

She tried to ignore the little pang in her heart. "So?"

"So I don't want to see you get hurt again."

Too late for that. She already knew she was going to miss Nate after he left. A lot. Despite their disagreements, she'd felt more alive in the past three weeks than she had since before Mark died.

She moved toward her father and slid the box on the counter between them. "The last time we talked about this, you said you were praying for a new man to come into my life. And you seemed to think Nate might be the answer to that prayer. Don't you like him anymore?"

"Of course I like him. I think he's a fine, decent man with honor and principles. But aside from the fact he's not going to be here long, I'm also getting the feeling he has some issues. You have enough of those yourself without taking on someone else's."

Too late for that, too.

She leaned on the counter. "He'd had a tough life. But he's dealing with his baggage."

"Have you dealt with yours?"

"You mean as far as Mark is concerned?" She pressed her finger against a stray cookie crumb that must have eluded her last night when she'd cleaned up for the day.

"Among others."

"Not entirely. But I'm working on them."

He eased a hip onto the stool. "Chicago is a long way away, Lindy. You ready for a move like that?"

She looked up. "No."

"Because of me?"

"What?" She blinked at him.

"You don't have to hang around forever babysitting an old man, you know. I could handle the Mercantile on my own now, with a little part-time help."

She forced her lips into a smile. "Trying to get rid of me?"

"You know better. But I don't want to hold you back, either."

"You're not what's holding me back."

"Didn't think so. Wanted to check, though. You making any progress with the man upstairs?"

Sighing, she propped her elbow on the polished wood and dropped her chin in her palm. "Not enough. But I've started reading the Bible again."

"I noticed." He reached under the counter, pulled out the small book with the familiar black cover, and set it next to the jumbled box of tuna. "I found this in the sunroom. Figured it was a positive sign." He checked his watch. "Looks to me like it's past time for lunch. Why don't you grab a sandwich and take a walk out to The Point for an hour? Nice spot for reading." He eased the book with the embossed gold cross closer to her fingers.

Subtlety wasn't her father's strong suit.

But his suggestion had merit. It was a beautiful day. And spending an hour with the Lord at The Point held a lot of appeal. Maybe it would help her sort through some of the issues her father had referenced.

"Okay." She hefted the box of tuna and set it on the floor at the end of an aisle. "I'll finish this when I get back."

"No hurry. I'm not expecting a run on tuna fish." He grinned at her.

She grabbed a turkey sandwich and a soda from the deli case, tossed them in a bag, picked up her Bible and started toward the door.

"Lindy…"

At her father's summons, she turned, hand on the knob.

"Everything will work out the way it's supposed to. And you don't have to solve every problem by yourself. He's on your side." He gestured toward the Bible in her hand. "You just have to put your trust in Him, especially when life's hard to figure out."

Lindsey nodded and pushed through the door, the merry jingle of the bell following her as she struck off for the hidden trailhead. Her dad was right. But trust didn't come easily for her anymore. That was why she carried the Beretta, tucked snug and secure in the concealed holster at her waist or kept close at hand behind the counter. Why she'd been wary when a grungy, road-weary Nate had shown up at the Mercantile that first day. Why she was fighting to save The Point from a developer who appeared to be ethical and honest, but who could end up destroying her cherished headland.

And as she circled the dental office and began to follow the faint trail that led to Starfish Bay Chapel, she wondered if even the Lord could restore the trust that had been shattered on that deadly night three years ago in Sacramento.

Tugging his phone off his belt, Nate plucked a dead blossom from the pot of flowers beside the stone bench and gazed out over the quiet sea off The Point, letting the peace and solitude of this place seep into his soul. He'd rather not take the call. But it was Clark again. And when a man who lived by email resorted to the phone, you answered.

Especially if you were toying with a proposal that would require his approval.

"Hi, Clark. What's up?" He put the phone to his ear, sat on the bench and stretched his legs out in front of him.

"Have you checked your email today?"

"This morning. Why?"

"What's the tally now?"

"More than five hundred."

"How are you answering the questions about donations?"

He frowned. "What questions?"

"Have you been reading the emails?"

"Some of them. But I have limited access to the internet here. I've been skimming through a few here and there."

"Well, start reading them. If we're getting questions about donations, you must be, too. People want to know where they can send money to help save The Point."

"Wow. I didn't expect that."

"It's quite a compliment. When people are willing

to shell out cold hard cash to save a place they've never seen because of words you've written, you know you've hit a home run. So where are we supposed to direct these people?"

"I have no idea. There is a Save the Point committee, but I don't think it's been formally organized or anything."

"Then tell them to get on the stick and set something up. If they want to take advantage of this outpouring of generosity, they need to strike while the iron is hot."

"I'll pass that on."

"You working on your next piece?"

"The research is finished."

"Excellent. Let me know how it's going. And get back to me on the donation question."

As the line went dead and Nate slid the phone back on his belt, he caught a glimpse of a slim figure emerging from the woods.

Lindsey.

Perfect timing.

A smile curved his lips as he followed her progress. Her head was bent, as if she was deep in thought, and she seemed oblivious to the wind that was tossing her hair around her face.

Only when she drew within fifty feet of the bench did she look up.

Her mouth formed a silent O and her step faltered before she picked up her pace again.

By the time she joined him, she was smiling, too. "I didn't expect to see you here."

"Great minds and all that." He scooted over and patted the seat beside him. "I saved you the best seat in the house."

She settled onto the concrete bench, depositing a

paper sack and a book with a gold cross on the cover between them. "Lunch hour."

He eyed the book as she dug into the sack. "Looking for answers?"

Her hand stilled for a minute, and then she drew out a sandwich. "Yeah. I have been for three years. Want half? It's turkey." She held up the plastic-wrapped offering.

"No, thanks. I ate a little while ago. Nothing that healthy, though. I'm addicted to the Orchid's French fries."

"That can happen." She opened her sandwich.

"I have some good news. I just talked to my editor. They're getting questions from readers who want to know where to send donations to help save The Point."

She stared at him. "You're kidding."

"Nope. Are you set up to handle that?"

"No. But we can be. I'll call my tax guy as soon as I get back. This is fantastic!" A flicker of excitement sparked in her eyes, reminding him of the old days. The first such spark he'd seen since his return. "I told you your piece would have an impact. You have a talent for that kind of writing. Maybe you should consider doing more of it." She lifted the sandwich toward her mouth and shot him an expectant look.

That wasn't a topic he was ready to talk about. With his editor—or Lindsey. Shifting the spotlight back to her, he tapped the cover of the book. "So is this helping you find your answers?"

The sandwich froze in front of her mouth for an instant before she took a bite—and gave herself an excuse to stall in the name of good manners.

Nate wasn't surprised. He'd been uncomfortable at first yesterday, when she'd pushed him to talk about stuff he'd never shared with anyone. But even as a kid, she'd had a way of listening that made you feel as if nothing else mattered, that nothing in the whole world was more important than what you had to say. She hadn't lost that knack. Or the ability to radiate empathy.

Today he wanted to return the favor. Offer her the same sympathetic ear.

And perhaps find answers to some of his own questions—about her.

After taking far longer than necessary to chew the mouthful of turkey and bread, she washed it down with a swig of diet soda before she responded. "Not as many as I'd like. And maybe I'll never find them. As Dad reminded me today, part of faith is trusting in the Lord—especially when things happen that you don't understand."

"That's not easy."

"No." She examined her sandwich, then set it back on the plastic wrap.

"I read the articles about your husband. And about the foundation set up in his name. Did the fund ever top half a million?"

"Yes. By a couple hundred thousand. So some good came out of the tragedy, at least." She broke off a piece of crust. Smashed it into a little ball in her fingers. "But it didn't bring Mark back."

There was no answer to that.

"One of the articles mentioned you'd been injured, too."

A spasm of pain flickered over her features, and she looked out over the sea. "Yes."

"How badly?"

Her throat worked as she swallowed. A few faint beads of perspiration broke out on her upper lip. Her chest rose and fell more quickly as her respiration grew shallow.

He watched, shaken and contrite at the realization that even three years later, memories of the incident could induce physical symptoms of trauma.

"Lindsey." He touched the clenched fist that lay in her lap. "I didn't mean to upset you. Forget I asked."

More silence.

Finally, she drew a shuddering breath and turned to him. "You told me yesterday you'd never shared the bad stuff in your past with anyone. I haven't, either. Not even my dad. Not all of it. But maybe I need to." She unclenched her fingers and ran them over the Bible beside her. "Maybe I have to let go of my hate and anger and resentment in my heart before there will be room for the Lord. Before I can heal."

"Maybe." What did he know? He was no theologian. Or psychologist. He was just a man who wanted to offer an old friend the same understanding and support she'd given him yesterday when he'd bared his soul.

A friend who was rapidly becoming much more.

Enough to make him rethink his future.

He moved the Bible and the sandwich he suspected she wasn't going to finish to his other side. Scooted close. Took her cold hand.

"I don't know where to start." The tremor of unshed tears was thick in her voice.

"Why don't you go back to the very beginning? Tell me about Mark. How you met."

A subtle easing in her taut posture confirmed he'd made a wise suggestion. Often it was easier to start with good memories and work up to the bad ones.

The faintest smile tugged at her lips. "He came to Starfish Bay on a fishing trip with some of his cop buddies. I was on summer vacation from my teaching job, and he stopped in at the Mercantile for a candy bar—and stayed all afternoon. He spent most of the rest of his trip fishing for dates instead of salmon and steelhead."

She looked out over the ocean, her eyes focused on the past rather than the shimmering water. "I had dinner with him a few times, but I tried to be practical. What were the chances he'd continue to pursue me once he went back to Sacramento? But he did. Anytime he had two consecutive days off, he was here. The sisters kept a room ready for him at the Orchid. And his persistence paid off. I ended up falling in love with him."

"And you got married at the chapel?"

"Yes. It was a day a lot like this one." She scanned the quiet sea, the blue sky, the clouds billowing in the distance. "Perfect. But from the beginning, I worried about the dangers of his job. He worked in the roughest part of town, and I prayed for him every day. He always downplayed the risks, always reminded me he was well trained. After a couple of years I worried less. And that's when it happened."

He stroked his thumb over the back of her hand but remained silent. Knowing there was nothing he could say to make the retelling any easier for her.

"The irony was, he wasn't even on duty that night. We'd gone to a fundraising dinner for Big Brothers. I wasn't feeling well, so we left early. As we walked to our car in the parking garage, we heard two men arguing. I didn't pay any attention to what they were saying, but Mark must have heard some words that alerted him it was more than a simple disagreement. He handed me his suit jacket, told me to stay where I was and walked toward them. The younger guy had this wild-eyed look, like he was strung out on drugs, and he pulled a knife. I'll always remember seeing that glint of light off the blade."

Her breath hitched, and Nate touched her hair, smoothing it back. Wishing he could wipe these memories from Lindsey's brain. But the sad truth was, they would be with her forever—as his would be with him. The best he could offer was comfort…and perhaps something deeper, down the line, if things progressed as he was beginning to hope they might.

"I remember Mark reaching for his off-duty weapon. But the younger guy rushed him. Mark's back was to me, and the next thing I knew he'd doubled over. I screamed. Ran toward him. He fell. I launched myself at the guy. I kicked him. Pulled his hair. He punched me in the stomach. Threw me off. My head hit a car bumper and I fell. Right next to Mark. Everything was blurry, but I could see the blood. Too much blood. It covered his whole shirt. Then the guy leaned over me. I thought he was going to stab me, too. Instead, he grabbed my purse, yanked my engagement and wedding rings off my finger and pulled Mark's wallet out of his jacket pocket."

Nate looked down at her bare ring finger. He'd wondered why she didn't still wear her wedding ring. But he'd never suspected a reason like this.

He started to reach for her. But her final broken, whispered words stopped him.

"I remember listening to his running footsteps receding in the distance. And I knew, even before we were found and the paramedics came, that Mark wasn't going to make it. And neither was our b-baby."

Shock ricocheted through him.

"You were pregnant?"

She dipped her head, and he felt a drop of moisture fall onto the back of his hand.

"I'd just taken a home pregnancy test that d-day. Mark was in a rush when he got home from work, and I decided to wait until the n-next morning to tell him. It was his day off, and I thought we could spend it celebrating. But he n-never even knew."

Another drop of moisture hit the hand that covered hers, and her shoulders began to shake.

Railing against the cruelty and injustice of a world where innocent people suffered and died, he shifted sideways to straddle the bench and pull her into his arms, his hand cradling her head as it lay against his chest. *Lord, why did you send down such misery on this wonderful woman?*

No answer came. None was expected. If God was listening, he'd tuned Nate out long ago. And in light of all that had happened to Lindsey, it was no wonder she was having difficulty connecting with the Almighty, too.

He held her as ragged sobs tore through her and his T-shirt grew damp. He held her while the sun dipped behind the gray clouds that had scuttled in and a shadow fell over The Point. He held her until her tears subsided and the first raindrops began to fall.

When she at last eased away to dig a tissue out of her pocket, she kept her head down. "Sorry. It's been a long time since I cried like that."

"I'm the one who's sorry." He smoothed back her hair, searching for words that would ease her pain. But what could he say that would comfort a woman who'd watched her husband bleed to death? Who'd lost her unborn child after a vicious, senseless attack?

The rain picked up, and he groped behind him to

rescue the Bible he'd placed there. As his fingers closed over it, a comment Reverend Tobias had once made suddenly flitted through his mind. It had been a few days before Christmas, not long after he'd heard his parents arguing—and sensed the perfect little world he'd occupied for the past few months was about to disintegrate. He'd sought out this place of refuge, where he and Lindsey had spent so many happy hours, not expecting to find anyone there.

But Reverend Tobias had been adding a few final touches to the crèche in front of the chapel. Though the pastor couldn't have been more than sixty, he'd seemed like one of the ancient sages to Nate, with his patrician features, kindly eyes and thinning gray hair. And what Nate had liked best was how he'd treated the questions of an eleven-year-old with the same gravity and thoughtful consideration as those of the senior members of the congregation.

On that day, he'd listened as Nate had poured out his angst and asked why God didn't save his tattered family. The man hadn't offered any platitudes. Or quoted any Bible verses. Or told Nate to pray. Instead, he'd put his arm around that young boy's shoulders and said a few short sentences that now flashed through Nate's mind.

"I don't know why, Nathaniel. But I absolutely believe God does. And I also believe someday, when you look back on this bad time, you'll see how God used it to mold you into a fine and honorable man who is going to make this world a better place. That will be my prayer for you."

In hindsight, Nate could see some logic in the minister's reply, though it had fallen on deaf ears twenty-five years ago.

But how could God ever use what had happened to Lindsey for good?

The very question she, too, seemed to be struggling with.

"You know, they never did catch the second guy."

Lindsey's words brought him back to the moment, and he looked down at her. She was still trembling in his arms as she reached for the Bible. He relinquished his hold on it.

"They got the man who killed Mark, though. He'll be in prison for a long time." She tucked the Bible close to her chest. "He didn't know his contact's name. It was a drug deal." Her voice quavered again, and when she lifted her chin, her tear-ravaged face and the desolate sadness in her eyes twisted his gut. "Sometimes I dream about the baby I lost."

He touched her cheek. "You never told anyone about that? Not even your dad?"

"No. If Mark couldn't know, I didn't want anyone else to know, either."

"Yet you told me. Why?" He thought he knew, but he wanted to hear it put into words.

She studied him, her expression pensive. "I don't know. It just felt...right."

Good enough. For now.

Taking her hand, he swung his leg over the bench and drew her to her feet. As the random drops of rain intensified, he scanned the sky. "We'd better head back fast or we'll get caught in this storm."

She tucked the Bible under her arm and twined her fingers with his. "I feel like I've been caught in a storm for three years."

He could relate. But his storm had lasted a lot longer. Yet as he set a fast pace toward the hidden trailhead that would lead them back to town, he had the oddest feeling the sun was about to peek through.

And for the first time in a very long while, he experienced an emotion long absent from his life.

Hope.

Chapter Twelve

"So what do you think?" Nate regarded Jarrod as the boy finished reading his piece on children who'd lost parents. He'd dived into it on Sunday morning, and for the past two days he'd left his room at the Orchid only to eat and pay a quick visit to Lindsey at the Mercantile.

"It's awesome." The youngster looked up from Nate's laptop at the table they were sharing in the coffee nook.

"Did you see the credit line?"

"Yeah." Jarrod's gaze flickered back to the words at the bottom of the last page: *With special thanks to Jarrod Peterson for his research assistance.* "You think people will like this as much as the one on The Point?"

"Hard to say. But if you and I like it, that's all that matters."

"Yeah. Hey, can I show this to my mom?"

"Sure. I'll email you a copy. But remember, my editor hasn't seen it yet, so there could be some changes. I wanted you to read it first, though."

The boy's chest puffed up. "You know, I've been thinking, maybe I could be a writer someday."

"No reason you couldn't be." And that was true. His reading and writing skills had improved significantly in the time Nate had been working with him. Writing hadn't even been on the agenda, but Jarrod had decided to summarize articles he read—and he'd done an excellent job. According to Lindsey, his math skills had also taken a quantum leap.

"Your mom's here, Jarrod." Lindsey leaned around the counter and called out to him.

He checked the window as she pulled in. "Okay. I'm coming." He rose and gathered up his books—including the one Lindsey had been working with him on before they'd piqued his interest in reading by making him a research assistant. A bookmark stuck halfway through suggested he'd picked it up again, with far better results.

At the threshold of the coffee nook, he paused. "So when are you leaving?"

"Probably sometime next week."

"I'll see you again then, right? Even though today was my last tutoring session with Ms. Collier?"

"You bet. I wouldn't leave without saying goodbye. Besides, I have to tell you what my editor says about our article."

"Right." He fiddled with the books in his arms. "Would it be okay if I emailed you once in a while after you go back to Chicago?"

"I'd like that."

"Okay." He lifted his arm in farewell and backed away. "See you around."

Seconds after the bell over the door jingled, Lindsey joined him. "He's like a different kid. You did a great job with him, Nate."

He watched Jarrod jog toward his mom's car through the plate-glass window, his step upbeat, a smile on his face. Odd. For years, he'd put himself in the line of fire, seeking meaning and worthiness and redemption by risking his neck. But none of those efforts had filled up the empty place inside him. Yet risking his heart by helping a young boy…by writing the piece on The Point…by sharing his secrets with Lindsey…by reconnecting with his past—and with God…had put him on the path toward a better future.

Not what he'd expected when he'd heeded the call to return to Starfish Bay—but then again, there'd been a lot of surprises on this trip.

He shifted his attention to one of them. The warmth in Lindsey's eyes infused him with the same glow he'd felt as a kid whenever she'd beamed her approval after he'd signed on for one of her scary adventures. Like the cliff-hanging hike down to Agate Beach—or so it had seemed to his eleven-year-old eyes as he'd watched her scuttle over the rocks like a crab while he'd crept along at sea-turtle pace. Yet by the end of the summer, his confidence bolstered, he'd become as adept as she was at maneuvering through the jagged boulders.

Fingering the stone in his pocket, he smiled at her.

She gave him a quizzical look. "What are you thinking?"

"About how you pushed and prodded me way outside my comfort zone as a kid."

The corners of her lips lifted. "You were a bit of a wimp in those days. But you turned out okay."

"Thanks at least in part to you."

She dismissed his comment with a shrug. "Don't give me too much credit. My motivation was more selfish than altruistic. I didn't want you to slow me down." Shifting her weight, she shoved her hands in her pockets, her tone growing pensive. "But maybe you were the smart one, after all. Sometimes caution is good."

The steady look she directed at him confirmed what

he'd already begun to suspect. That despite the confidences she'd shared with him on Saturday at The Point, she had qualms about taking their relationship to the next level.

Given her history—and the temporary nature of his stay in Starfish Bay—he understood why.

He also knew that addressing her concerns had to be his top priority in the next few days.

As he opened his mouth to respond, the phone behind the counter began to ring.

"That's probably the attorney in Eureka who's drawing up the paperwork for our Save the Point organization. He said he'd call about now." She took a step back, her relieved expression telling him she was glad their conversation had been cut short. "As soon as I get the green light I'll let you know where to direct your readers who want to contribute."

Without waiting for a reply, she rounded a shelving unit and disappeared.

Nate let her go. For now. He understood that the heartaches she'd endured had made her wary. That getting involved with another man in a dangerous profession—who also happened to live halfway across the country—was a major hurdle.

But he was putting together a plan he hoped would eliminate those obstacles.

And he prayed it would open the doors to the life he believed God had called him to on that desert night a world away from Starfish Bay.

As the cameraman from the San Francisco TV station wandered around The Point searching for the best shooting angle, Lindsey forced herself to take a deep breath. In a minute or two, the reporter standing off to one side and jotting in a notebook would expect her to face the lens and give viewers an articulate, poised response to her questions.

She turned away, toward the sea, and wiped her palms down her jeans as she fought back a wave of panic. Saying yes to the request for an interview when the news team had shown up at the Mercantile soon after Nate departed had been a no-brainer. The more publicity they got about the Save the Point campaign, the better. And if Nate could venture far outside his comfort zone by penning that heartfelt piece for the *Tribune*, the least she could do was speak on camera for three or four minutes.

Except the last time she'd been up close and personal with a reporter had been right after Mark's death. And it had not been a positive experience.

But this was different. And it was for a good cause. She could do it. She *had* to do it. The whole Save the Point campaign had been her idea. She couldn't drop the ball.

Too bad Nate wasn't here, though. His mere presence would calm her, and she'd—

"You okay?"

At the familiar resonant baritone behind her, she whipped around. Blinked. Was the man standing a few feet away real or some wishful apparition she'd conjured up? She blinked again. Much to her relief, Nate didn't vanish. "What are you doing here?"

"I left my flash drive on the table at the Mercantile, and when I went back your dad told me about the news crew. I thought I'd drop by and see if you could use a little moral support."

"Yes." She choked out the word. Without thinking,

she reached for his hand, twined her fingers through his and held on. Tight.

For a moment, he seemed taken aback by the impulsive gesture. But then he gave her a reassuring squeeze. "Your fingers are cold."

She checked over his shoulder. It appeared the cameraman, who was now conferring with the reporter, had found his spot. Her pulse kicked up a notch and she tightened her grip.

"I don't know if I can pull this off. The only other time I've faced a camera was after Mark was k-killed. The reporter cornered me as I left the hospital, and when he pushed for details about what happened in the parking garage I ended up falling apart in front of thousands of viewers. Instead of apologizing for being a jerk, he was aggravated I ruined his exclusive interview."

A muscle tensed in Nate's jaw. "Some of those broadcast types are insensitive, arrogant hotshots. I ran into a few in the Middle East. But I've caught some of her interviews on TV since I've been here." He inclined his head toward the female reporter, still in conference with the cameraman. "I don't think you need to worry. My guess is she's going to give this the David and Goliath treatment. I would, in her place."

"You think so?" Lindsey sized up the reporter.

"Yeah. I do. Just talk to her the way you talked to me about this place. Let your passion come through. And don't forget to mention the tax-exempt foundation. Might as well get as many donations as you can out of this." He winked at her.

Lindsey felt some of the tension in her shoulders ease. "Will you hang around during the interview?"

"That was my plan. Unless my presence will make you more nervous."

She met his gaze. "In this case, it would help keep me calm."

The slight flicker in his eyes told her he'd caught her deeper meaning. That apart from this interview, he did make her nervous. And they were going to have to talk about that. Soon. She didn't know how much longer he was planning to stay, but it couldn't be more than a couple of weeks. And while they'd shared a great deal with each other, while they'd connected at an elemental level, while the spark between them was strong, she had no idea if they were going to be able to deal with all of the challenges—and obstacles—that stood in the way of deepening their relationship once his stay here was over.

"Ms. Collier? We're ready."

Lindsey's pulse tripped into double time again, and after one more squeeze of her hand, Nate released her fingers with a smile.

"Knock 'em dead." He gestured off to the side. "I'll be over there."

"This way, Ms. Collier. We want to use the chapel as a backdrop."

As the reporter ushered her to a small rise overlooking The Point, with the weathered chapel and cerulean sea behind her, Lindsey watched Nate fade into the background. As the camera began to roll she focused on him, taking comfort in his encouraging smile.

By the third question, however, she was on a roll as she let the passion she felt for The Point bubble to the surface.

When she finished, she checked on Nate again, who gave her a grin and a thumbs-up.

She wanted to thank him. But the reporter had more questions, background information she needed to help her develop an introduction for the story. Once it became apparent Lindsey would be tied up a while, Nate pointed to the hidden path, lifted a hand in farewell and strolled toward the woods. By the time she was finished, he was long gone.

Just as he would be in a couple of short weeks.

Only he'd be a lot farther away than the Orchid Motel.

That thought sent her spirits into a tailspin.

"Can we offer you a ride back to town?" The cameraman called out the question as he loaded his equipment in the back of their rented Suburban.

"No, thanks. I know a shortcut through the woods."

With a wave, he climbed behind the wheel and pointed the vehicle down the road.

Once it disappeared around a curve, Lindsey wandered over to the bench, wishing Reverend Tobias was still around to offer his trademark words of wisdom. All her life, up to and including the day she'd married in this very spot, he'd known exactly the right thing to say, no matter the situation.

As she sat, a snippet of the sermon he'd preached at her wedding suddenly surfaced, taking her by surprise. She'd been so caught up in the euphoria of the ceremony, her hand clasped in Mark's, that most of what her pastor said had been a blur.

Odd that now, years later, his conclusion would echo in her mind with such clarity.

Loving is always a risk. Always. Life holds no promises. Blue skies can darken in a heartbeat. Landscapes can shift overnight. That's why it takes courage to love. But the gift of love, given and received, is well worth

*the risk. Because love can, to paraphrase a famous
aviator, allow us to slip the surly bonds of earth and
touch the face of God.*

Lindsey's vision blurred. When Reverend Tobias had
spoken those words on that joy-filled day, she'd heard
only the upbeat message. The part about love moving
one to a higher realm. As it had.

The concept of risk and the tenuous nature of happiness hadn't even registered.

It did now, though.

Because loving Nate was a risk.

Yet could she let him walk away, now that it was obvious the connection that had sealed their friendship as
kids was stronger than ever?

Rising, Lindsey surveyed the sea, then traced the
length of the tall, weathered steeple. Despite the turmoil
of her thoughts, she did know one thing: to make this
relationship work she needed both courage and trust.

But as she trudged toward the hidden path that would
take her home, she wasn't certain she had enough of
either to overcome her fear and induce her to take a
second chance on love.

"You want another refill?"

At Genevieve's query, Nate checked out his half-
empty mug sitting on the Orchid Café counter.

"How many have I already had?"

"Lost count at number three. We have a bottom-
less cup, and I know you like your java, but seems like
you're going to be floating out of here soon. You hang-
ing around for any particular reason?" She used the pot
in her hands to indicate the booth in the corner, where
Lindsey, her back to them, was in deep discussion with
yet another reporter.

No use trying to fool the sisters. They were on to him. He'd been lurking around Lindsey ever since her TV interview at The Point two days ago, trying to catch her alone. So far, no go. By design, he suspected. Nor was she answering her cell or returning his messages.

And until they had a long and serious talk, his hands were tied. No sense moving forward with his plan if she'd gotten cold feet about them.

Talk about a discouraging thought.

"Never mind. I can figure it out."

At Genevieve's comment, he transferred his attention back to her. "Getting five minutes alone with her is as impossible as resisting your sister's blackberry cobbler."

The older woman chuckled. "She's been busy getting the Save the Point organization set up and dealing with the media. Did you know we already have more than $10,000 in donations? Amazing what a little publicity will do. Not to mention that fine article you wrote that kicked the whole thing off. But if you want my honest opinion—" she leaned closer and dropped her voice to a conspiratorial whisper "—I think she's running scared. You have the look of a man on a mission. That can be intimidating to a woman."

"Not to a woman who's interested."

"Oh, she's interested, all right." Genevieve straightened up. "But she left Starfish Bay once for a man she loved, and it ended badly. Can't be easy for her to consider turning her life upside down again."

"Maybe I'm not expecting her to."

She gave him a speculative look. "You tell her that?"

"I have some things to work out first. But I need to

find out how serious she is before I put the wheels in motion."

"I see your dilemma." Genevieve eyed the corner booth again. "Tell you what. They seem to be wrapping things up over there. And I see Frank Martinez waiting to waylay her. You wait in the office. Lillian's gone to Crescent City for a few hours, so you'll have it to yourself. I'll get you your five minutes with Lindsey. The rest is up to you."

He grinned. "I owe you for this."

"I'll keep that in mind." Giving him a saucy wink, she waved him toward the back of the café.

After checking to confirm that Lindsey was still engrossed in her discussion, he slid off his stool and slipped through the door that led to the office where he'd borrowed Lillian's internet connection.

Less than ten minutes later, intent on whatever errand Genevieve had concocted, Lindsey pushed through the door and crossed to the desk, scanning the littered surface.

Nate reached for the door. Gave it a slight push. Planted himself in front of it as it clicked shut and Lindsey swung around.

"Hi." He folded his arms across his chest.

"What are you… Did Genevieve ask you to…oh!" As she put two and two together, she tried to back away. But the desk blocked her.

"We need to talk."

"I've been busy."

"We can make this work."

She gripped the edge of the desk behind her. Although her eyes widened at his cut-to-the-chase comment, she remained silent.

He took a step toward her and softened his voice. "Do you *want* it to work, Lindsey?"

Her throat contracted as she swallowed, and distress tightened her features. "I haven't had two minutes to call my own since The Point thing started to accelerate. I need some time to think things through."

"Maybe you just need to listen to your heart."

"Doing that got me into trouble once."

He moved closer. Close enough to tell she was quivering. "Did it? That would suggest you regret marrying Mark, and I don't think you do. If you had it to do again, knowing how it would end, would you have wanted to miss the life you had with him—and the love you shared—no matter how brief?"

She stared up at him. Moistened her lips. "No." The word came out in a broken whisper. "But risking that kind of loss again...I don't know if I have the courage to do that."

"I think you do. I think you know love is worth it. And that's where we're headed. At least I am. And I'm hoping you are, too."

His next move hadn't been part of his strategy. And while he knew it might not be the smartest thing he'd ever done, Nate followed the urging of his own heart.

Resting his hands on her shoulders, he leaned down and kissed her.

Even as he made contact, he told himself to keep it quick and gentle. A mere touching of lips, lingering just long enough to test the waters. He didn't want to compound this possible mistake by letting things get too heavy—despite the strong urge to tug her close and give her a true demonstration of the depth of his feelings.

Except Lindsey's response changed everything. He'd

expected her, at best, to accept his kiss. He hadn't expected her to melt against him, throw her arms around his neck and return the kiss, holding nothing back.

One thing combat coverage had taught him was to remain flexible. Adapt to sudden changes.

So he adapted. Enthusiastically.

How much time passed, Nate had no idea. But when Lindsey at last eased back and he searched her flushed face, inches from his, he wished this moment could last forever. Because as he held her in the shelter of his arms, he knew with absolute certainty this was where he was meant to be. That after years of searching, after logging hundreds of thousands of miles all over the world, he'd come home at last.

Before he could speak, however, she wiggled free, slipped around him and made a beeline for the door.

He turned, but stayed by the desk. "Lindsey."

She hesitated, her hand on the knob, and risked a peek at him. Her hair was mussed, her cheeks flushed, her respiration uneven.

"We still need to talk."

"I know." The words came out breathless. "But not today."

With that, she slipped through the door and closed it behind her.

Nate didn't follow. He didn't have to. This little rendezvous hadn't been designed to eliminate the obstacles in their path—only to find out whether Lindsey cared enough about him to make eliminating them worthwhile.

And when he finally strolled toward the door, stopping in front of the Paul Bunyan souvenir mirror on the office wall to wipe a smear of lipstick off his cheek, he grinned. They might not have talked much just now. But he had his answer.

It was time to put his plan into action.

Right after he took care of one other important piece of business.

"Did your editor really like it?" Jarrod leaned forward in his chair, eyes alight.

Nate smiled. The eagerness and enthusiasm on the boy's face was more than enough payoff for the hours he'd spent working with him. "He loved it. I couldn't have done it without you, though, and I told him that."

The youngster beamed.

"Here you go." Cindy exited the house onto the deck carrying two glasses of lemonade and set them on the round patio table where he and Jarrod sat.

"Nate's editor liked our story, Mom."

"That doesn't surprise me. You both did an incredible job." She sent a grateful smile his way, and Nate acknowledged it with a slight dip of his head. "Now I'll leave you two gentlemen to finish up your business. I still have another load of laundry to do."

As she disappeared back through the sliding door, Jarrod took a sip of his lemonade and furrowed his brow. "You know, I thought this summer was going to stink. Dad always tried not to travel as much when I was off school, and me and him would bum around together a lot. When he did go out of town, Mom thought up lots of cool stuff for us to do, too. Then everything changed." He traced the partial ring of condensation on the table, using his finger to complete the circle. "I never thought I'd be happy again. But this summer turned out okay, after all."

Yeah, it had. For him, too. Thanks in part to the boy

sitting across from him, who'd helped him confront a lot of his own issues from the past—and write an article that had been as therapeutic for him as it had been for his young student.

But most of all thanks to Lindsey, who'd pushed him beyond his comfort level, into emotional territory he'd avoided for too many years. And who'd stolen his heart all over again in the process.

"So are you leaving soon?"

At Jarrod's question, he forced himself to refocus. "I'm not sure of my timing yet."

The boy swirled the ice in his glass, keeping his gaze on the opaque liquid. "It's too bad you have to go back. Starfish Bay is a nice place to live. But I guess Chicago is more exciting."

Not anymore.

"It has its good points, like any other place." He kept his response noncommittal and changed the subject. "So tell me what book you're reading now."

He listened as Jarrod launched into an enthusiastic recap of the latest adventure novel Lindsey had recommended, three levels higher than his current grade. The boy's reading skills had soared in the past few weeks. Another gratifying outcome of their tutoring sessions.

As they finished their lemonades and Cindy showed him out, Jarrod followed him to his car, then stood awkwardly, hands in pockets as they said their goodbyes. At the last second, though, the boy surprised him with a quick hug, then backed off and dipped his head to hide the telltale blush as he spoke.

"Thanks again. For everything. I sure wish you were staying."

Throat tightening, Nate squeezed the boy's shoulder. "I appreciate that."

And as he climbed into his car, he couldn't help hoping that if all went as he planned, a certain shop-keeper would respond with an impulsive hug of her own—and a similar sentiment.

Chapter Thirteen

Lindsey eased through the door of the Orchid Café, which was more packed than usual for Saturday lunch, the customers shoulder-to-shoulder in the small foyer area as they waited for seats. A quick scan told her Nate wasn't among the diners who'd already been served, confirming what the absence of his car in the parking lot had already implied—he wasn't around. For a man who'd said he wanted to talk, he was certainly making himself scarce. And he couldn't have lost interest. Not based on that kiss two days ago in the Orchid office.

At the mere thought of that cozy encounter, a flush of embarrassment warmed her cheeks. What in the world had come over her? Nate might have initiated the embrace, but she was the one who'd taken it to the next level, despite her reservations about their future. Talk about acting completely out of character. Not that he'd seemed to mind, although…

"Lindsey? Is that you back there?"

At Genevieve's query, Lindsey waved at the older woman. "Yes. Quite a crowd today."

"I've got a counter spot if you're alone."

Truth be told, the only thing she was hungry for was

Nate's company. But maybe Genevieve could enlighten her about his vanishing act.

"That'll work."

Edging sideways through the crowd, she tried not to step on too many toes. Once she emerged from the crush, she followed Genevieve to the counter and slid onto the one empty stool.

"My goodness. I can't recall ever having such a busy Saturday, except the time that movie company came up here to film for a few days. That was back when you were still in Sacramento. Best I can tell from doing a little eavesdropping, most of these folks heard about The Point in the media and came up to take a look. Might be a few donations out there." She winked and gestured to the Save the Point brochures Lindsey had arranged to have printed. "I'm handing them out with every bill. What's the tally now?"

"Close to twenty-five thousand, as of last night."

"Mercy! That's a chunk of change. And to think it all started with that piece Nate wrote."

The perfect opening.

Lindsey made a project of unwrapping her silverware from the paper napkin. "I haven't seen him in the past couple of days."

"Oh. I thought you knew. He left this morning for Chicago."

The fork slipped out of her fingers and clattered to the floor.

Heart pounding, she slid off the stool and bent to retrieve it. Nate was gone? Without a word?

A sense of déjà vu swept over her. Surely history wasn't repeating itself.

"No. I hadn't heard that." She grabbed the fork and retook her seat.

"Here, let me replace that for you." Genevieve gave her a knowing look, tugged the fork from her fingers, and pulled a clean one from below the counter. "He said he had some business to take care of. I don't think he plans to be gone for more than a day or two."

Lindsey let out a relieved breath.

He was coming back.

"You didn't think he'd up and leave without saying goodbye, did you?"

At Genevieve's slightly reproving tone, a wave of guilt crashed over Lindsey. "No. That wouldn't be like him."

"It surely wouldn't." Genevieve retrieved a sponge from below the counter and swiped at an imaginary speck on the spotless surface, using that as an excuse to lean close and speak more softly so the diners on either side of Lindsey wouldn't hear. "But he will be leaving soon. Unless someone gives him an incentive to stay. As my grandma Wilson always used to say, when the Lord sends an opportunity your way, have the good sense to recognize it."

"Genevieve! Tony's going down for the third time." Lillian bustled over, a stack of menus in hand. "Unless you want to lose the best kitchen helper we've ever had, you better get back there and pitch in. I'll handle the hostess duties. But if this keeps up, we're going to have to hire more help!"

Without waiting for her sister to respond, Lillian hurried toward the front door.

"Duty calls." Genevieve pulled out an order pad. "What'll you have, Lindsey?"

"Scrambled eggs to go with my scrambled brain?"

The older woman grinned at her rueful inflection. "I'll bring you a chicken Caesar salad. You missed the boat on breakfast." She wrote on the pad, tore off the sheet and winked. "Just don't miss the boat with Nate."

With that, she pushed through the door to the kitchen.

"Lindsey!"

Her mind still on Nate, it took Lindsey a few seconds to shift gears after Susan Peroni called out to her. As she turned toward the mayor, the woman said a few words to her husband, who continued toward the door while his wife joined Lindsey at the counter.

"What's up, Susan?"

"I had a call from Louis Mattson while Dale and I were eating. He saw your interview on the news, and he's been reading the articles that have been cropping up about The Point. The PR backlash has apparently made him rethink the project. He asked if we could defer making plans for a citizen vote at our meeting next week and instead let him come back to discuss the project again with residents. I'm going to send an email out to the council members this morning. And we'll need to put up flyers around town and at the Mercantile. I expect we'll have another full house." Twin creases appeared on the woman's brow. "I have a feeling he's going to withdraw his proposal for a development."

Though tempted to cheer, Lindsey did her best to maintain a neutral expression. "If he does, we'll survive."

Susan shot her a disgruntled look. "I know this is what you wanted. And I love The Point, too. But sometimes love isn't reason enough to preserve something. Not if there are greater benefits in letting it go."

"I'm not certain there are."

The mayor regarded her. "Did you know Janice is thinking about closing her gallery?"

Lindsey blinked. "No."

"It's not public knowledge. Janice mentioned it a few days ago when I stopped in to buy one of those hand-made greeting cards she sells. There's not enough business in Starfish Bay to cover her expenses and provide her with a living wage. But there might be if we had an upscale resort nearby."

Susan let that sink in for a moment before she continued. "And Janice isn't the only one struggling in this tough economy. It seems to me part of our responsibility as council members is to do everything we can to make this community not only an appealing place to live, but a viable place to do business. Don't you?"

Guilt tugged at Lindsey's conscience. "Yes. But on the flip side, don't we have a responsibility to preserve the natural beauty of this place for future generations?"

"Assuming there's still a town here for future generations to live in. Dennis is having financial issues at the fishing camp, too. So is Jaz." Susan adjusted the strap **of** her bulging shoulder purse. "Well, I'll get the notices printed up and drop off a few at the Mercantile. Spread the word about the meeting, okay?"

"Sure."

As Susan wove through the tables, Lindsey swiveled back to the counter. Her gaze fell on the placemat, which featured a slogan the sisters had written soon after they opened the café.

Wish upon a star in Starfish Bay—where dreams come true.

Was Susan right? Were the dreams of a lot of people—like Janice and Dennis and Jaz—about to go belly-up? Would Inn at The Point save them?

Yet if it did, other dreams would die. Starfish Bay Chapel and the headland—a touchstone for many residents—would disappear. Should those irreplaceable assets be sacrificed on the altar of economic prosperity?

A few weeks ago, her answer would have been an unequivocal *no.* But if Janice and Dennis and Jaz were in trouble, others were, too. Even the Mercantile was feeling the pinch. So where did her loyalties lie—with the town, or with the touchstone?

For the first time, a niggle of doubt undermined Lindsey's resolve to save the chapel and The Point. Strange, when the tide of opinion now appeared to be turning in her favor.

Genevieve slid her salad in front of her, but as Lindsey picked up her fork and poked at the chicken, her appetite evaporated. What was she supposed to do? Stick with her original plan and fight the development? Or put practicality above principle?

And she was equally confused on the personal front. She'd kissed Nate two days ago, sending a clear message she cared for him. She'd panicked this morning when she'd thought he'd left. Yet she also felt panicked about pursuing a relationship with him. Would he end up in a body bag on some distant battlefield? Would she find herself alone in Chicago, as she had in Sacramento, forced to once again pick up the pieces of her shattered life and start over?

Lindsey closed her eyes and gave up any pretense of eating.

Lord, please show me what to do so I don't make a mistake with either Nate or The Point that I'll spend the rest of my life regretting.

* * *

"That's an interesting proposal, Nate. And I'm impressed you came all the way back here to present it in person…at your own expense."

One side of Clark Gunn's mouth hitched up as he tacked on the final four words, and Nate flashed him an answering grin. His editor was notoriously tight with the *Tribune's* money—and his own—an idiosyncrasy often joked about by the reporters and staff. His legendary frugality was, in fact, one of the reasons Nate had made this quick trip. This discussion was too important to be relegated to phone or email, and he wanted Clark to know that.

"So what do you think?" Nate's pulse tripped into double time, much as it had whenever things got dicey during a dangerous recon assignment in Afghanistan. There'd always been a risk he could be shot down on one of those missions. Just as his proposal could be shot down on this one.

"You sure this is what you want?"

"Yes."

Clark studied him. "I'm not going to ask, but I'm guessing there's a woman involved. Someone you're willing to change your life for after a handful of weeks."

His boss had been a formidable investigative reporter in his day, with rock-solid intuition. Nate wasn't surprised the man had come to the correct conclusion. But neither did he intend to provide details.

"There's more to the story than that."

"Good to know. You've never struck me as the impetuous type. And I'd hate to see you make such a dramatic change only to later regret it." Clark tapped his pen on the desk. "You sure you wouldn't rather extend your leave a few weeks, think things through more thoroughly? I could arrange that."

"Thanks for the offer. But I've already thought this through."

"Okay." He leaned forward in his chair, set his pen down and propped his elbows on the desk. "I'd rather have what you're offering than nothing at all. But this isn't a decision I can make. I need to run it by Frank. He might want to talk to you, too. He's out until tomorrow afternoon, though. How long are you staying?"

Nate had assumed Clark would need to confer with the managing editor on this. But he hadn't counted on extending his stay. He had an appointment on Wednesday on the West Coast he didn't want to postpone.

"I was planning to fly out tonight. I can delay thirty-six hours. No more."

One of Clark's bushy gray eyebrows rose. "She must be some woman." When Nate didn't respond, the older man chuckled and picked up his ringing phone. "I'll let you know as soon as I talk to Frank. And we're running the piece on kids who've lost parents next week. It was even better on a second read-through. Should resonate with a lot of people."

"Thanks." Nate rose.

"Any more think pieces in the hopper?" He put the phone to his ear.

"Yeah. Depending on what Frank says."

Lifting a hand in dismissal, Clark barked his last name into the phone. Nate's cue to leave.

Less than five minutes later, he emerged onto Michigan Avenue. The cacophony of big-city sounds he'd once found energizing, the tall concrete towers that had once seemed glamorous, could no longer compare to the quiet of a small northern California town where the highest thing in sight was a soaring redwood.

He was even immune to the interested glance of a passing twenty-something woman wearing a fashionably short skirt and skinny high heels. Compared to Lindsey? No contest. Clark had been right about the motivation for his proposal.

And if all went well here and in Arcata on Wednesday, the major obstacles Lindsey had to their relationship should be history.

"You're awful quiet today, Lindy."

At her father's comment, Lindsey looked up from the doodles she'd been drawing on a pad of paper to find him lugging a box of canned tomato sauce from the Mercantile's storeroom.

"I can do that, Dad."

She started to rise from the stool behind the counter, but he waved her back down. "I've been working in the garden all summer, honey. My biceps are in excellent condition." He set the box down next to the shelf that needed restocking and flexed his muscles.

It was his balance, not his upper body strength, that concerned her. And he seemed to read her mind.

"Sit, Lindy." He motioned her down. "I'm learning to compensate for this limp. And I'm doing fine. You need to stop worrying. About me, anyway."

She sank back down. Knowing, from his caveat at the end, that more was coming.

Brushing off his hands, he walked over to her. "So how come you're so quiet? Thinking about the meeting tomorrow?"

"Yeah." She planted her elbow on the counter and set her chin in her palm. "Things aren't quite as clear-cut as they once were. Susan told me several businesses are seriously hurting. Janice might even have to close."

"I heard a rumor to that effect myself." He rested his forearms on the opposite side of the counter and leaned forward. "Life's never simple, is it?"

"No."

"I guess all we can do is weigh the consequences and then make the best choices we can with the information we have."

"I don't know what the best choice is in this case. The long-term consequences aren't clear."

"They rarely are."

He glanced down at the pad in front of her. She followed his gaze, only to discover she'd been doodling hearts. As a flush rose on her neck, she repositioned her hand to cover the telltale scribbles.

To her surprise, he didn't comment. "Maybe you should see what that developer has to say tomorrow night. You might be able to strike a compromise."

"I'm not holding my breath."

"You could pray about it, though. And about that." He gestured toward the pad in front of her. "Compromise might go a long way toward resolving that situation, too."

"Aren't you the one who raised a caution flag about Nate not long ago?" A defensive note crept into her voice.

"I did. But I've been doing a fair amount of praying about you two. And I've come to believe God brought him here for a reason that includes you."

She swallowed past the sudden lump in her throat. "I can't imagine leaving Starfish Bay again. Or you."

"Love requires give and take, Lindy. And Chicago

isn't that far away by plane. We wouldn't have to be strangers."

"But this is home. And much as I loved Mark, not a day passed when I lived in Sacramento that I didn't miss Starfish Bay."

"It would always be here, waiting for you to come back."

"Maybe not the way I remember it." Her throat tightened, and she stared out the window toward The Point. "Why does life always have to be hard? Just when I was settling back in, Nate shows up and changes everything."

"Like Mark did."

"And look how that turned out."

"Are you sorry you met him?"

She angled back toward her father. "Nate asked me the same thing."

"And?"

"No. But I've learned that the happy endings I used to believe in sometimes only happen in fairy tales."

"Depends how you define happy ending, I guess. They come in a lot of different forms." He straightened up and gave her a gentle smile. "When your mom died, everyone called it tragic. They said she was too young. That it wasn't fair. And for a long time I bought into that and was angry at God for taking her from us too soon. But you know what? The truth of it is, I was blessed to find someone who loved me so deeply. Who gave me a beautiful daughter I cherish. Who graced my life for fifteen glorious years, the memory of which still fills my heart with joy. If you ask me, that's a happy ending."

Steadying himself on the counter, he leaned closer and patted the hand she'd placed over the telltale hearts.

"Give it to God, Lindy. And don't rush Him. He'll send you the guidance you need in His own time."

As her father limped back over to the box of tomato sauce and began to restock the shelf, Lindsey moved her hand aside and inspected her unconscious doodles. Some of the hearts were single. Alone and separate from everything else. But most overlapped.

A sign—or wishful thinking?

She had no idea.

Maybe her dad was right, though. Maybe she was rushing things. Perhaps, if she gave this a little time, she'd get some clear guidance on what to do about The Point—and Nate.

Unfortunately, waiting for anything—guidance included—had never been her strong suit. Indecision annoyed her. Since she hadn't a clue about how to solve either of her problems, however, what option did she have? Because she *was* certain about one thing.

She didn't want to make the wrong decision about either the touchstone from her past or the man who could be her touchstone for tomorrow.

Chapter Fourteen

The town hall was packed.

Again.

From her place behind the long table in front, Lindsey scanned the crowd. Unlike the last meeting, which the media had ignored, this one had attracted the attention of several local and San Francisco TV stations and newspapers, as well as a network affiliate. Shoulder-held minicams were already panning the room for crowd shots as residents settled into their chairs, and reporters with pens poised over their notebooks had claimed first-row seats.

Louis Mattson was there, too, along with a couple of his colleagues. They were seated off to one side, conferring quietly.

The only person she didn't see was Nate. As far as she knew, he still hadn't returned from Chicago.

Maybe he wasn't coming back, despite what he'd told the sisters.

She didn't want to believe that, but perhaps, once back in familiar territory, he'd decided that while it had been nice to reconnect with his childhood friend, there wasn't a place in his life for her, after all. And how could she blame him? Except for that one kiss, she hadn't given him much encouragement. For all she knew, he was already planning his next overseas assignm—

Susan banged the gavel on the table, and Lindsey jumped. "This meeting is called to order."

As the mayor welcomed everyone, then introduced Louis Mattson, Lindsey forced herself to focus. The fate of Starfish Bay Chapel and The Point merited her undivided attention. She couldn't let personal problems distract her.

Mattson stood and moved in front of the three easels his assistant had placed beside the head table, each one holding a large covered presentation board. His smile was genuine, his stance relaxed. If he was angry about the bad PR Lindsey had helped generate, he gave no indication of it.

The man had polish and class, no doubt about it.

And his attire, like last time, was impeccable. Custom-tailored suit, based on the fit, knife crease in the slacks. Crisp white shirt. A blue and gold silk tie Lindsey was certain cost more than the fanciest outfit in her closet.

"First, thank you, Mayor Peroni, for giving me a chance to return and speak to the residents of Starfish Bay. I must say, I had no idea our proposal would provoke such controversy. But I salute everyone who went to bat to protect what many of you consider an irreplaceable community asset. A touchstone."

He smiled and slipped one hand in the pocket of his slacks. "If the gentleman who wrote that excellent piece is here tonight, I'd be honored to shake his hand after the meeting. And I'd also be honored to shake the hand of council member Lindsey Collier, who I understand spearheaded the Save the Point campaign."

When he glanced toward her, Lindsey felt a flush creep up her neck. But again, his demeanor was sincere rather than spiteful or angry.

"All of the publicity that's been generated, particularly that first article, reminded me of a touchstone in my own life. I was born and raised in rural Missouri, and one of my favorite childhood memories was spending a day in a beautiful spot we called Fern Spring. It was the kind of place families gathered for picnics on summer Sundays, with a deep swimming hole and a tire swing, located in a fern grotto that always seemed to stay cool, even on the hottest August day. And trust me, Missouri can get mighty hot."

As the man walked toward the center of the room, leaving the easels behind him in the hushed hall, Lindsey found herself caught up in his story—as were the rest of the attendees, based on their rapt expressions.

"I used to get back to Missouri once in a while. And whenever I returned, I always took a trip to Fern Spring. To that touchstone from my childhood. But last time I went, five or six years ago, it was gone, a victim of the far-reaching tentacles of urban sprawl. There's a subdivision there now called Fern Valley, and the spring's been diverted underground to the nearby river. As I stood there, grappling with the realization that this wonderful place from my youth had disappeared forever, I felt as if someone had ripped a hole in my heart. So I understand the importance of touchstones—and of preserving natural beauty."

If this was a PR ploy, Lindsey was falling for it hook, line and sinker. And a quick survey of the crowd told her the rest of the residents were, too.

Mattson crossed back to the easel. "For that reason, I asked my site engineers and architects to take another look at the proposal for Inn at The Point. And I'd like to show you what they came up with." He nodded to his colleague, who flipped back the cover on one of the presentation boards to reveal the original design for the inn, with a modified version beside it.

"As you can see, we've taken the design from three stories to two to give it a lower, less intrusive profile that will blend even more seamlessly into the natural landscape. We've also relocated it a bit to hide it more from 101, leaving intact much of the view of the headland from the road."

He moved to the second easel and his colleague flipped back the cover on that board. "We took this aerial view of The Point during our initial site study. For orientation, here's 101." He traced the highway with his finger. "As you know, we'd like to purchase the entire headland. But we always intended to keep most of the land in its natural state. Rather than asking Starfish Bay residents to take that on good faith, however, we're willing to build language into our purchase agreement that designates the area between these lines—" he indicated a large swath of forest between two dotted red lines, "—as a nature preserve, subject to further development only with the approval of the Starfish Bay Town Council. We would also grant public access for recreational use."

Gesturing to his colleague, he walked over to the third easel. His assistant flipped that cover back as well, revealing an artist's rendering of a small white chapel very similar to the one on The Point.

"And finally, the chapel. Our structural engineer tells us the current chapel has serious instabilities. In addition, it's located on land we need for the inn. So we would like to offer a compromise. We'll salvage what we can from the current chapel, including the bell and as much of the interior as possible, and construct a miniature version of Starfish Bay Chapel on the south end of inn property. It will be set in its own garden, and we'll use it as a wedding chapel. But we'll also make it available to residents for special-occasion use."

He returned to the center of the room. "And now, I'd be happy to answer any questions or address any further concerns."

As a few people rose and made their way to the microphone in the center aisle, Lindsey looked around the room. One sweep of the faces told her everything she needed to know.

Louis Mattson would get his inn.

A pang of sadness echoed in her heart. Yet in good conscience, she could no longer stand in the way of this development. Every concern raised had been addressed as sensitively and thoroughly as possible short of scrapping the project and leaving The Point pristine. But even if that happened, the chapel would continue to deteriorate. Either way, The Point was going to change.

Just as life did, no matter how hard one tried to hold on to the past or the present.

Five minutes later, as the last resident behind the microphone took his seat, Susan spoke again. "If there are no more questions, I'd like to ask anyone who still has an objection to this project to please raise your concerns now."

Lindsey checked with Frank. He gave a slight shake of his head. She moved on to Susan, who was watching her. And shook her head, too.

She saw Susan take a deep breath as she turned

back to the audience. When no one spoke, she smiled at Louis Mattson. "Mr. Mattson, I believe we have a go. And on behalf of the council and the residents, please accept our thanks for your consideration and responsiveness. This meeting is adjourned." She banged the gavel.

The media surged toward the developer and the mayor, but a number of people joined Lindsey, too, including the sisters, her father, Frank and Clint, who'd taken on a lot of the grunt work for the Save the Point campaign. She looked to him first, knowing that as a naturalist, he'd have strong feelings about the outcome.

"How do you feel about this?"

"In light of what could have happened, I view this as a win-win."

That made her feel better.

"You did fine, Lindsey." Genevieve patted her on the back. "Why, if you hadn't gotten everyone all riled up and raised a stink about this, that developer would never have gone back to the drawing board."

"That's true," Lillian concurred as Frank bobbed his head.

Her father beamed an approving smile at her. "Just goes to show that one person—or a handful—really can make a difference. I'll wait in the back until you're ready to leave."

While she chatted with other Save the Point committee members, Louis Mattson joined her, waited his turn, then shook her hand. He was as charming and genuine to her as he'd been in front of the crowd in the meeting, and she felt even more comfortable with the outcome as he released her hand and shifted around to take another question from a reporter.

That's when she caught sight of Nate, shouldering through the crowd toward her.

He'd come back!

And now, with the situation at The Point resolved, she had to face the next critical question.

Where did the two of them go from here?

If the answer was forward, she knew that just as with The Point, compromise would be required.

After much prayer and thought, she was prepared to do her part.

But would Nate meet her halfway?

Nate knew the instant Lindsey spotted him. Her expression went from surprised to joyous to uncertain in a heartbeat.

But if all went as he planned, he'd be erasing that uncertainty in the next thirty minutes.

The small cluster of people around her dissolved as he approached, and Lindsey ignored the knowing wink that passed between Genevieve and Lillian as they melted into the background. But it was impossible to disregard their soft, delighted titter when Nate went straight to her, took her hands, and gave her a kiss on the lips right in front of the whole town.

"I missed you." The muted words were spoken close to her mouth, the whisper of his breath warm on her cheek.

"I m-missed you, too."

"Good." He eased back slightly and smiled down at her. "I got here in time to catch most of the presentation. Are you happy with the outcome?"

"Yes. The town benefits economically, and the development has the lowest possible environmental impact. You can take a lot of credit for that. Your touchstones piece had a big impact on Louis Mattson. Were you here when he talked about that?"

The sudden self-conscious ruddiness in his neck gave her his answer before he spoke. "Yes. But you were the one who inspired me to write it. And share it." He took her hand and perused the milling crowd. "Do you need to hang around here?"

"No. But Dad's waiting for a ride…"

"No, he's not." Her father eased through a gap in the crowd. "I bummed a lift from Clint once I spotted Nate. Three's a crowd and all that." He leaned over and gave Lindsey a quick peck on the cheek, then winked at the two of them over his shoulder as he headed for the tall naturalist who was waiting in the back of the hall.

"Can I interest you in a visit to The Point?"

At Nate's question, she shot him a surprised look. "In the dark?"

"I have a flashlight in the car. And there's a full moon tonight. We can celebrate a happy ending."

He wasn't just talking about The Point. Happy as that outcome was, it wouldn't generate the undercurrent of excitement that was charging the air between them. Or fill his eyes with warmth and hope. Or produce that ever-so-slight tremor in his fingers when he took her hand.

No, he had an entirely different happy ending on his mind.

But she hadn't expected to have to deal with this tonight. Hadn't psyched herself up for the serious conversation they needed to have. Hadn't organized her thoughts or…

"Hey." He gave her fingers a gentle squeeze. "While I wouldn't be in the least opposed to another kiss in the moonlight, I'm not going to rush you, okay? But I do have some news I want to share. Will you trust me on this?"

As she looked at the childhood friend who'd returned from the past and staked a claim on her heart—and her future—she gave the only possible answer.

"Yes."

"Watch your step." As they circled the chained-off entrance to the road that led to The Point, Nate hit the auto locks on his car and pocketed his keys. Flashing the beam of his light ahead of them, he took Lindsey's hand. She hadn't said much on the short drive from the hall, and he could feel the tension emanating from her. Not positive signs.

On the other hand, he hadn't imagined the flash of relief—and welcome—in her eyes when she'd spotted him at the hall.

Things would be okay.

They had to be.

Even if he hadn't gotten exactly what he'd wanted from the *Tribune*.

The road was dark, the trees shrouded in shadows, but once they emerged onto the tip of the headland the flashlight became unnecessary and he clicked it off. The moonlight gave the chapel an ethereal glow and silvered the sea, the shimmering orb so bright even the canopy of stars was dimmed by its luster.

"Wow." Beside him, Lindsey slowed. "I don't come out here much at night. It's stunning, isn't it?"

"Very." He led her to the bench. "Let's sit for a little while and I'll tell you my news."

She did as he asked, and after one more sweeping scan of the view she focused on him.

Given the significant role it had played in both

their lives, this spot had seemed like the obvious place to share his news. But now Nate wondered if it had been the best choice. Bright as the moonlight was, he couldn't see her features as clearly as he'd like to. He wouldn't be able to read her emotions in her expressive eyes.

Then again, maybe that was a blessing. If he saw withdrawal or uncertainty, he might lose heart.

Putting doubts and second guesses aside, he wove his fingers through hers and plunged in. "I've been busy the past few days."

"So I heard. I didn't know you were planning to go back to Chicago."

He should have told her about the trip. But he hadn't wanted to lie about the reason for it. Nor raise false hopes. "It came up pretty suddenly. And I didn't expect to be gone more than a couple of days. But the managing editor was out of town and I ended up needing to talk with him, which delayed my return."

"New assignment?"

He felt her pull back. Emotionally, if not physically.

"You might say that. One I initiated. Because of you."

He heard her breath catch. Felt her grow still as she spoke. "What do you mean?"

A breeze ruffled her hair, and he lifted a hand to touch the soft, gossamer strands that were luminescent in the moonlight. "Since the day I left Starfish Bay, this spot has been my touchstone. The place I measured the world against. And everywhere else I went, everything else I did, came up short. I was not only a man without a country, I was a man without a purpose. That cold, hard fact slammed home to me as I lay on that bombed-out road in Afghanistan, watching brave soldiers die as I wondered, 'Why me?'

"A few weeks later, something—or Someone—guided me back here. Desperation, not high expectations, compelled me to follow that call. I knew I had to fill the gap in my soul, and this was the only place where life had ever felt right. I guess deep inside, I hoped coming back might make it right again. And it did. Thanks in large part to you."

He eased closer to her on the bench, keeping her hand firmly in his. "Truth be told, I didn't know if you'd still be here when I decided to come back. And I wasn't sure that mattered. I was more interested in revisiting the past than rekindling a relationship with an old friend. But once we reconnected, I realized a lot of my happy memories of this place were due to you. And I didn't want those memories to be confined to the past. I wanted to make new ones with you. At the same time, I recognized there were obstacles. So I've done my best to remove them."

Lindsey gave him a cautious look. "How?"

"I went to Chicago and asked the *Tribune* to restructure my position. Instead of being a full-time reporter, I proposed doing a syndicated column twice a month and taking on periodic special reporting assignments. I also visited with the chairman of the journalism program at Humboldt University in Arcata this afternoon to discuss a position as an adjunct professor, teaching courses on field reporting and investigative journalism, starting in January. For the most part, I got what I wanted from both parties. That means I can make my base in Starfish Bay—and we can explore this relationship at our leisure."

Nate hadn't expected Lindsey to throw her arms

around him and declare her undying love. Given her history, he'd known she'd want to take this slow and easy. But he'd hoped his news would be met with more than a wide-eyed stare.

And as the silence between them lengthened, broken only by the muted crash of the waves on the rocks below The Point, he suddenly wondered if he'd mis-read her kiss and made a huge mistake.

Nate had changed his life for her. Because he hoped they had a future together.

It was mind-boggling.

And scary.

And amazing.

His lips flexed, as if he was trying without success to smile. "Maybe I took too much for granted."

"No." Lindsey tightened her grip, wishing she could see into his eyes. But the moon was behind him, shad-owing his face. "I think we have possibilities, too. I just didn't see how we'd get around the obstacles. I figured I'd have to move to Chicago if we wanted to make this work. And I had reconciled myself to doing that. It never occurred to me you'd..." Her voice trailed off as the magnitude of what he'd done began to fully register. "Nate, you have a life in Chicago. And a great career with the *Tribune*. I never expected you to give that up."

"I have no life in Chicago. I live in a studio apart-ment—when I'm in town. It's a place to stay, nothing more. I have no ties to the city. And I still have a career with the *Tribune*. Plus a new one, teaching at the col-lege level."

"But Starfish Bay is a tiny town. In the middle of nowhere. Can you really be happy here?"

There was no hesitation in his response. "I already

am. I've loved this place since I was eleven. And I'm falling in love with the best friend I ever had, who happens to live here. That makes it perfect." He shifted, and even before he continued, a sudden tension in his posture put Lindsey on alert. "But there's something else I have to tell you."

The bubble of happiness growing inside her froze at his somber tone, and she braced herself. "What?"

"I mentioned that I'd gotten almost everything I wanted. But there was one concession I wasn't able to negotiate, hard as I tried. The *Tribune* is willing to try this new arrangement for a year, until management has a feel for how my column is going to be received long-term. If all goes well, combat assignments will be off the table. But for now, they've reserved the right to send me overseas to do additional combat coverage. In fact, they want me to leave later this month for a two-week assignment in Iraq."

The bottom fell out of Lindsey's stomach.

Nate would be back in the line of fire.

"Can you live with that situation for a year?" He tightened his grip on her hand.

Could she? Could she let herself fall in love with the man beside her, give him her heart, and risk having things end in tragedy as they had with Mark? While she'd reconciled herself to the notion of moving to Chicago, to making the kind of compromise her father had rightfully suggested was part of love, she'd hoped Nate would reciprocate by pulling back from combat coverage.

Instead, he'd taken the initiative on moving, leaving combat coverage on the table instead. In a mere handful of days he'd be leaving for a war zone.

And maybe end up coming home in a body bag.

A sudden chill rippled through her, and she shivered as she looked over the sea. Fog was rolling in, fast and thick, obscuring the light from the moon, hiding the twinkle of the stars, covering the landscape in a formless gray shroud. Darkening the night.

Beside her, Nate clicked on the flashlight, stood and drew her to her feet. "We better leave before this gets dangerous. I don't want us taking a header off the side of the cliff."

Without waiting for a response, he hustled her toward the road. She didn't argue. After spending most of her life on the coast, she knew how treacherous fog could be. It could disorient in a heartbeat.

Kind of the same effect Nate's announcement had had on her.

They didn't talk as they hurried toward the road, steps ahead of the swirling fog. Even then, Nate rushed her into the car and set off for her house, intent on delivering her safely and getting back to the Orchid before driving became too hazardous.

When he stopped in front of the house she shared with her father, he started to get out to walk her to the door. But she restrained him with a hand on his arm as tentacles of fog wrapped themselves around his Acura.

"Don't take the time. You'll need every minute to get back to the Orchid before we're socked in. Would you call me after you get there, so I know you're safe?"

"Yeah." She started to slip out of the car, but he grabbed her hand. "You never answered my question about whether you can live with my situation for a year. And maybe that's an answer in itself. If it is, I want you to know I'm willing to quit the *Tribune*."

She was shaking her head before he finished. "It wouldn't be fair for you to make all the sacrifices."

"I don't consider anything I do for us a sacrifice."

Her throat tightened. "But what if you do all that, make all these radical changes in your life, and things don't work out?"

"I'm willing to take that chance." He held her gaze for a moment longer, then released it as he checked out the diminishing visibility. "Sleep on it, okay? We'll talk tomorrow. I'll call you in a few minutes."

With a nod, she closed the door and slipped into the house, watching as his taillights were swallowed up by the fog.

Praying for the courage to put her trust in him—and the Lord—and take a second chance on happily ever after.

Chapter Fifteen

He should have taken time for dinner.

As Nate pulled into the Orchid parking lot and set the brake on his car, he rubbed at the knot in his stomach. He'd grabbed a bagel in the airport this morning, eaten nothing but a tiny bag of peanuts on the West Coast flight, and pulled off the highway for a fast-food burger en route to his meeting in Arcata. Once that was finished, he'd sacrificed dinner to head straight back to Starfish Bay, determined to make it in time for at least part of the meeting.

No wonder his stomach was protesting.

Or maybe the twisting in his gut had more to do with Lindsey's lack of enthusiasm for his news than lack of food.

Punching her number in his phone as he slid out of the car, he watched the fog obscure even the light beside his room, less than ten feet away.

She answered on the first ring. "Are you there?"

"Yes. And not a minute too soon. Visibility is almost zero." He grabbed his overnight bag from the trunk, set the locks and felt his way along the car toward his door.

"Nate, I'm still trying to take in everything you told me tonight. It was a little overwhelming. I'm sorry if—"

"Lindsey." He fitted the key in the lock and pushed the door open, eying the bed. He needed to lay flat, give the kinks in his stomach a chance to work themselves out. Besides, if she was going to back out of this relationship, he didn't want to hear the bad news tonight. "Let's put off any discussion until tomorrow, okay? I'd rather talk in person. Plus, I'm beat. I've been on the go since five this morning."

"Okay." Her tone was subdued, and he could imagine her catching her lower lip between her teeth. "But can I at least say thank you? Not only for everything you did, but for caring enough to do it?"

"Sure." He tossed his bag onto a chair and stretched out on the bed. Better. "But I'm not sure your gratitude is deserved. Remember how you once told me your motive for pushing me beyond my comfort zone as a kid was selfish? Mine is, too. If things go the way I hope they do, I get you. I figure I'm the real winner in this deal."

A soft chuckle came over the line. "I like an honest person."

"Vice versa. So let's plan on having an open, honest discussion first thing tomorrow morning. Assuming the fog's lifted, how about meeting for breakfast at the Orchid? About seven?"

"I'll be there. Good night, Nate."

"Good night."

The line went dead. Nate tapped the end button on his cell, set it beside him and linked his fingers behind his head. He needed food and he needed sleep. But the former was unappealing, and the latter would probably be elusive.

It was going to be a long night.

* * *

Lindsey shoved her tangled hair out of her face, slid the mug of milk into the microwave and peered at her watch in the dim kitchen. Two-thirty in the morning. And she'd clocked no more than thirty minutes of fitful sleep. Max.

Maybe the hot chocolate would help. Warm milk was supposed to induce sleep. And it was better than the Ambien she'd almost become addicted to after Mark died. No way was she going down that road again.

But if she got involved with Nate, she'd worry every time he left on an assignment. Sleepless nights could once more become the norm. Fatigue could set in. Desperation could lead her back to the pills.

Yet another reason to back away from this relationship.

The microwave emitted a beep, and she quickly jabbed at the off button. No reason to wake her dad just because *she* couldn't sleep.

As she stirred powdered chocolate into the mug, the distant wail of a siren broke the stillness. An accident in the fog, no doubt. The roads were treacherous in daylight; at night and obscured by mist, they could be downright deadly. Over the years, a number of people had lost their lives on the stretch of 101 south of town by driving too fast and missing a curve, or by sliding on wet pavement. But most residents knew better than to tackle these roads on a dark, foggy night. Especially at this hour. Must be someone unfamiliar with the area.

Lindsey wandered over to a window that gave her a view down the street, toward 101, and raised the shade. The fog had lifted somewhat, increasing visibility. But the weather was still dicey. Navigating the roads would be a gamble.

A gamble some driver had lost, she suspected.

To her surprise, the emergency vehicle didn't stop at the curvy section of highway south of town, however. Instead, the siren continued to grow louder. Flashing lights appeared in the distance. An ambulance emerged from the fog, traveling as fast as the weather allowed.

So much for her theory.

As it zipped past the intersection, siren blaring, she almost missed the ring of the kitchen phone. But when it did register, she dashed across the room and grabbed it, leaving a trail of hot chocolate splotches behind her on the pristine floor. Who in the world would be calling at this hour?

"Hello?" Her greeting came out in a rush of breath.

"Lindsey, I'm sorry to wake you, but I didn't know who else to call."

Lillian.

Lindsey's heart tripped at the panic in the older woman's voice. Lillian never lost her cool. The ambulance must be for Genevieve.

"It's okay, Lillian. What's wrong?"

"I wouldn't have bothered you, but he doesn't have any family I know of, and you two are so close…" Her words trailed off as someone else spoke in the background. Genevieve. She said something about the ambulance arriving.

Lindsey did the math. Genevieve wasn't sick. Plus Nate didn't have a family. That added up to big trouble.

Now it was her turn to panic.

"What's wrong with Nate?" Even as she spoke, she shoved her mug onto the counter and tore toward her room.

"We don't know." More noise in the background,

followed by male voices. "But the EMTs are here now, thank the Lord."

"What happened?" She set the phone on speaker and threw it on her bed, then grabbed for her jeans and shoved her feet into the legs.

"Genevieve heard a suspicious noise in the parking lot about half an hour ago. We investigated and found Nate slumped next to his car. He said he didn't feel well and needed to get to an emergency room. But he wasn't in any condition to drive. His face was gray and he was shaking. So we called 911."

Pulling a T-shirt over her head, Lindsey dropped to the edge of the bed and felt around with her toes for her shoes, trying not to hyperventilate. "Where are they taking him?"

A muffled exchange took place. "St. Joseph's. In Eureka."

"I'll follow the ambulance there. Would you let the EMTs know? Nate, too."

"Yes. Drive safe, Lindsey. The roads are bad. And call us when you have any news, okay?"

"I will. Thanks for letting me know." She pushed the end button, then fumbled the shoelace, her shaky fingers refusing to cooperate. Three tries later, she managed to tighten the loops of the bow.

Standing, she picked up her phone, then strode down the hall and tossed the cell in her purse. Keys in hand, she grabbed a jacket off a peg by the back door. Should she wake her father or leave a note?

Without wasting time debating the issue, she pulled a pen and piece of paper out of the drawer next to the telephone and jotted him a brief message. No sense both of them losing a night's sleep.

Sixty seconds later, as she backed out of the driveway, the ambulance whizzed past her street on 101.

Gripping the wheel, she pressed on the accelerator, barely paused at the intersection, then turned left on the highway. The ambulance had already disappeared around a curve. She increased her speed.

And as she followed the winding road that was as familiar to her as the rugged terrain of The Point, she didn't waste the long drive.

She used it to pray.

Acute appendicitis, requiring immediate surgery.

Lindsey gripped the arms of her chair in the ER waiting room as a nurse passed on the diagnosis. Thankfully, Nate had been coherent enough to authorize the emergency staff to share information with her.

"Did it rupture?"

"We're not sure yet."

"If it did, what are the risks?"

"A perforated appendix can result in peritonitis—basically, an infection in the abdominal cavity. That would be treated with intravenous antibiotics and require a longer hospital stay. There's a small risk of more serious complications like sepsis, where the blood carries infection to other parts of the body, but that's not something you should worry about at this point."

Easy for her to say.

"How long will he be in surgery?"

"Depends on what they find. Plan on an hour or two."

"Can I see him first?"

"He's already being prepped." The woman rose. "Let me direct you to the surgical waiting room. The doctor will look for you there when he's finished." She handed over a plastic bag. "The patient said we could give you his clothes and personal items."

Lindsey pushed herself to her feet, hoping her unsteady legs would support her. She took the bag, hugging it to her chest as the woman issued the directions.

Eight minutes later, she found herself in the deserted, chair-lined room. Choosing the nearest seat, she sank into it, still clutching Nate's things.

Was it only nine hours ago that she'd sat in the town hall as the fate of The Point was decided? Eight hours since Nate had dropped his bombshell about the dramatic changes he'd made in his life to accommodate her? Seven and a half hours since she'd let him drive away instead of throwing her arms around his neck and telling him she, too, believed they were meant to be together and was willing to take their relationship to the next level, no matter the risk?

Now he was headed for surgery.

Lindsey settled the bag on her lap, propped her elbows on her knees and dropped her head into her hands. She had to get a grip. An appendectomy wasn't a heart attack. And this kind of surgery wasn't usually life-threatening. He'd be okay.

Unless his appendix had ruptured and he got peritonitis. Or sepsis.

If he did, he could die.

Not on a battlefield, but right here in her backyard.

As that reality slammed into her, as she faced the stark truth, her stomach clenched. People didn't die just on battlefields. A dangerous profession might increase the chance of death, but a safe profession didn't insulate a person from mortality. Bottom line, loving was a risk.

And if she wanted to protect herself from that risk,

she'd have to write off romance. Period. Send Nate packing. Refuse to fall in love with him.

Except it was too late for that. She was already falling.

Hard.

Why else would she be shaking as badly as she'd been in the ER three years ago while she'd lain in the treatment room, waiting for word on Mark?

Why else would her stomach be twisting in fear that a doctor would walk through the door here, just as one had in Sacramento, and confirm what she'd already known in her heart—that the man who was the center of her world had died?

Why else would she be asking God to spare Nate so they could make those new memories he'd talked of last night at The Point?

The faint scent of Nate's distinctive aftershave wafted her way from the bag in her lap, and she eased the top open, glancing down as she took a long whiff. The worn jeans were familiar, as was the beige cotton shirt, rolled to the elbows. His wallet and watch sat on top of the pile, along with a handful of change. She squinted, shifting the bag around to better catch the light from the dim lamp on the other side of the room. Was that a rock?

Curious, she withdrew the small, translucent stone with the intricate white banding. An agate.

A faint memory niggled at the back of her mind, of a child's damp palm with this stone resting in the middle. Surf crashed in the background. A little boy's voice echoed in the recesses of her mind.

"I'll keep this forever."

And he had.

A literal touchstone to his past.

Throat tightening, Lindsey closed her fingers over the stone, leaned back and tipped her head against the wall.

That's when the empty place in the small of her back registered.

She'd forgotten her Beretta.

Panic surging, she shot back up. In the two and a half years since she'd become certified to carry, she'd never left home without it. The gun made her feel safe. Protected. Able to defend herself.

Yet she'd never needed it. And the odds were high she never would.

Another truth smacked her in the face. While the gun might keep her fear of physical assault at bay, it couldn't do a thing to alleviate the emotional fear that gripped her now.

Nor could it offer protection from the dangers of acute appendicitis.

A sob caught in her throat and she slumped back against the wall. Not long ago, she'd accused Nate of living in the past. He'd countered by declaring she was doing the same thing. That old fears were holding her back.

She'd denied it. But he'd been right.

Instead of leaving her fear and trauma in the past, she'd been letting them shape her present—and deny her the future Nate believed God had planned for them.

A future filled with love.

Tears streamed down her face, unchecked in the silent, lonely room. But as the eternal minutes crept by, as dawn's light at last began to seep around the edges of the closed blinds, as more worried families joined her in hushed vigil for their loved ones, she finally put her trust in God—and let go of fear.

* * *

A whisper of warmth hovered at his forehead. Soft pressure followed. The faint flowery scent that was all Lindsey tickled Nate's nostrils. And then she whispered the most beautiful words he'd ever heard.

"You better get well fast, Nate Garrison. Because I'm falling in love with you and I want to start making those new memories you promised me."

Maybe he'd died and gone to heaven.

On second thought, he felt too sick to be dead.

Fighting back a clawing nausea reminiscent of his one and only bout with seasickness, Nate tried to open his eyes. Failed. Forced himself to try again, shocked at the enormous effort it required.

But the reward was worth it. When at last he managed to pry open his eyelids, Lindsey's beautiful face was inches from his. Yet the fine lines at the corners of her eyes, her pallor and her shaky smile told him she hadn't had an easy time of it, either.

"Hi." She whispered the word, the taut line of her features easing slightly when his gaze connected with hers.

"Hi." He swallowed, willing the nausea to subside as he tried to orient himself. In his peripheral vision, he caught sight of an IV stand beside the bed. "I see I made it to the hospital."

"Barely."

He refocused on her, but she spoke before he could ask the question.

"Ruptured appendix. They're pumping lots of high-powered antibiotics into you to stave off peritonitis. Last time they checked, the antibiotics were winning."

Hoping to find a more comfortable position, he

shifted. A hot poker jabbed him in the abdomen and he froze, sucking in a sharp breath.

Lindsey frowned and touched his hand. "Do you need some more pain medication?"

He clenched the sheet in his fingers. "It couldn't hurt."

She started to reach for the call button, but he grabbed her hand. "Not yet. You have to answer a question for me first."

"Okay."

"Was I dreaming just now, or did you say you were falling in love with me?"

A soft flush suffused her cheeks. "You weren't dreaming. I had a lot of time to think—and pray—while I waited for you to get out of surgery. And I realized I'd been fooling myself all along. I could no more stop myself from falling in love with you than I could have refused to love Mark. Nor do I want to."

She leaned closer and touched his cheek. "And to answer the question you asked me last night at The Point, yes, I can live with your situation at the *Tribune* for the next year. Because I don't want to live without you."

A well of tension inside Nate, so deep he'd been aware of it only at some peripheral level, began to release. In its place, he felt a joy unlike any he'd ever known. Heady enough to dull his pain. "This calls for a celebration. Or at the very least, a kiss."

Lindsey grinned. "Are you up for that?"

He grimaced. "Honestly? No."

"I didn't think so." She pressed the call button. "But I expect a rain check."

"Count on it."

"In the meantime, I'll settle for this."

Once more she leaned close. Once more her lips brushed his forehead. Once more he closed his eyes.

And as she took his hand, her fingers warm and welcoming as they captured his, Nate decided Thomas Wolfe was wrong.

You could go home again.

And sometimes, it was even better than you remembered.

Epilogue

Three and a half months later

"Star light, star bright, first star I see tonight." Nate gestured to the east, where a lone star was beginning to glimmer in the dimming sky while the sun set behind them off The Point.

Lindsey smiled up at the man beside her, the childhood friend who had become much, much more in the months since he'd returned to Starfish Bay.

"There's another line to that rhyme, you know."

He draped an arm across her shoulders and grinned. "That's all I remember. And even that was dredged up from who knows where. My mom must have taught it to me. What's the rest?"

"I wish I may, I wish I might, have the wish I wish tonight."

"And what is your wish, Lindsey Collier?" With his free hand, he traced the curve of her cheek.

She leaned into him, savoring his touch, then shifted toward Starfish Bay Chapel. "That Reverend Tobias could be here to hold one last Christmas Eve service tonight."

Silence fell, broken only by the muted crash of waves and the caw of a gull. She'd spent so many happy Christmas Eves in the bough-bedecked church, joining other Starfish Bay residents to celebrate a birth that had changed the world. Now those candlelight services were gone forever.

And in a week, her own world would change, too. On January 2, Mattson Properties would begin dismantling the chapel and start construction of the inn. Although she'd reconciled herself to the inevitable months ago, it was still hard to say goodbye.

"I have a feeling the good minister is here in spirit. I can almost feel his presence. And hear him telling us to stop living in the past and make the most of the present." Nate tugged her closer, shielding her from the wind.

Lindsey smiled. "In his gentle way, of course."

"Of course. That's why his counsel was so effective. And unforgettable."

"I agree." She sighed and shoved her hands into the pockets of her jacket. "I guess we better head back. Dad's ham will be coming out of the oven soon, and Genevieve and Lillian are probably already at the house. Clint's going to stop by, too, since he's all alone for the holiday. Did I tell you he found a firm to develop an interpretive trail on the public-use area of the headland? That will be a great use for the money people donated to Save the Point."

"You mentioned some plans were in the works. I didn't know it was a done deal, though."

"As of yesterday. But you were engrossed in your latest column, and I didn't want to interrupt. Genius at work and all that." She grinned at him.

"Not quite."

"Absolutely." She wasn't about to let him downplay his talent. "You get more mail than any other columnist. As you should. And I predict tomorrow's piece will generate a phenomenal response. I loved your whole take on the criteria for a perfect gift—and how you worked in the reference to my snow globe. Which is front and center on our mantel, by the way." She squeezed his hand. "The *Tribune* is lucky to have you. And so am I."

The tender smile he gave her warmed her as thoroughly as sunshine banishes the chill after a storm. "You told me your wish. Now I'll tell you mine."

When he reached into the pocket of his jacket and withdrew a small box wrapped in silver paper, Lindsey's pulse skittered.

"Seems like history repeating itself, doesn't it?" He grinned as he led her toward the bench the developer had promised to save and reinstall beside the new chapel, tugging her down beside him as he sat. "Twenty-five years ago I gave the best friend I've ever had the snow globe you just mentioned to let her know how much she meant to me. Tonight I'd like to give the only woman I've ever loved a different gift—but the intent is the same."

As Nate handed over the small box, Lindsey looked into the deep blue eyes she cherished. Over these past few months, as he'd adjusted to his new life, she'd seen them flash with enthusiasm, soften with kindness and occasionally simmer with anger at injustice and callousness. Nate, as she'd discovered, was truly a man who lived the golden rule.

And he loved her.

With a depth and completeness that took her breath away.

She weighed the box in her hand, prolonging the moment, then slowly tore off the silver paper to reveal a dark blue velvet box. Fingers trembling, she flipped the lid.

A stunning marquis diamond ring blinked back at her, its sparkle putting the stars overhead to shame.

Joy bubbled up in her heart. Filled it. Overflowed.

She lifted her head and smiled up at him. "Yes."

Nate stared at her. "Wait a minute. This is way too easy. I had a whole speech prepared. I even had a plan B if you said no."

"I played hard to get long enough when you first came back. I didn't see any reason to keep you guessing. If you want me to withdraw that answer, though..."

"No way." He grabbed the box, removed the ring and slid it on the third finger of her left hand. "But I insist on delivering at least one part of my little speech." Taking her hands, he angled toward her. "I can't promise you tomorrow, Lindsey. We both know that's impossible. Life doesn't come with guarantees. But I can promise to love you with every fiber of my being for every single minute we're given as man and wife."

Moisture clouded her vision, and Lindsey put her arms around his neck to pull him close, overcome with gratitude for the unexpected gift of love that had graced her life and given her a brighter tomorrow.

"I'll make the same promise in return. And pray God grants us a long and happy life together. Because I want to grow old with you, Nate Garrison. I want to raise our children right here in Starfish Bay. I want to search for agates with them on our beach. And I want to tell them a story about a little boy named Nathaniel and a little girl named Lindsey who spent one magical summer together, slew some dragons and grew up to find their own happily ever after."

Nate grinned. "Sounds like a fairy tale."

"Except it's all true. Complete with the happy ending."

"Yeah, it is." His voice hoarsened, and he cleared his throat. "And the sooner the better for the happy ending, as far as I'm concerned. I checked with Mattson, and they're confident they can have the new chapel ready by spring. Ours could be the first wedding there. What do you think?"

"I think that would be perfect. And in the meantime—" she scooted even closer "—do you know what I think Reverend Tobias would say if he was here right now?"

"What?"

"Kiss the bride."

A chuckle rumbled deep in Nate's chest. "Who am I to argue with such a wise man?"

And as the stars twinkled above, as The Point kept watch, he claimed her lips in a Christmas Eve kiss to remember.

* * * * *

Dear Reader,

Welcome to Starfish Bay! *Seaside Reunion* is the first book in my new series for Love Inspired. I hope you enjoy visiting this charming spot on the northern California coast.

When I wrote this book, I intended it to be a stand-alone novel. But as often happens with my books, other characters appeared who asked me to tell their stories. So a series was born. Next up will be Cindy's story. You met her briefly in this book, when Nate and Lindsey joined forces to help her son, Jarrod, get back on track in school after the death of his father. Now a widow raising her young son alone, she has no interest in romance. But love often comes along when we least expect it.

In the meantime, I invite you to check my website at www.irenehannon.com for more information about my other books.

Irene Hannon

Questions for Discussion

1. Because of Lindsey's traumatic experience, she carries a gun. Do you agree with that decision?

2. Nate has returned to Starfish Bay because it holds happy memories for him. Have you ever returned to a place you loved? What was that experience like?

3. The notion of touchstones is important in this book. Are there touchstones in your life? Talk about one of them. Why is it so important to you?

4. Though Reverend Tobias is only seen in this book through the eyes of Lindsey and Nate, what is your impression of him? Have you ever met someone who, years later, can still touch your life? Why did that person have such a lasting impact?

5. Both Lindsey and Nate struggle to understand how a loving God can let bad things happen to good people. How do you deal with this question? Are there any particular Bible verses that have helped you make peace with this?

6. Who was your favorite character in the book? Why?

7. What was your favorite scene in the book? Why?

8. Nate had a very difficult childhood. How was that manifested in his adult life? Cite specific examples from the book.

9. Why do you think Nate has such strong and good memories of Lindsey?

10. Do you think it was realistic that Nate and Lindsey would reconnect so quickly after so many years? Why or why not?

11. Jarrod is having a difficult time coping with the sudden death of his father. In addition to struggling with schoolwork, what are some other ways a child might be affected by the loss of a parent? How might the surviving parent help that child cope?

12. Nate is angry when he finds Lindsey reading his touchstones piece. Do you think he overreacted? Why or why not?

13. When Nate sent his piece on touchstones to his editor, he was taking a leap far outside his comfort zone. Yet it led to good things. Have you ever taken a chance and done something that was uncomfortable? What was the outcome?

14. In the end, Lindsey concludes that love, like life, requires compromises. Do you agree? Can compromises ever hurt a relationship? If so, how?

15. How did you feel about the resolution of the situation with The Point? Were there any other good options?

INSPIRATIONAL

Wholesome romances that touch the heart and soul.

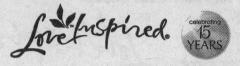

celebrating
15
YEARS

COMING NEXT MONTH
AVAILABLE JANUARY 31, 2012

HOMETOWN HEARTS
The Granger Family Ranch
Jillian Hart

THE LAST BRIDGE HOME
Redemption River
Linda Goodnight

SECOND CHANCE MATCH
Chatam House
Arlene James

ROCKY POINT PROMISE
Barbara McMahon

FALLING FOR THE FIREMAN
Allie Pleiter

A HOUSE FULL OF HOPE
Missy Tippens

Look for these and other Love Inspired books wherever books
are sold, including most bookstores, supermarkets, discount
stores and drug stores. LICNM0112

REQUEST YOUR FREE BOOKS!

2 FREE INSPIRATIONAL NOVELS
PLUS 2
FREE
MYSTERY GIFTS

YES! Please send me 2 FREE Love Inspired® novels and my 2 FREE mystery gifts (gifts are worth about $10). After receiving them, if I don't wish to receive any more books, I can return the shipping statement marked "cancel." If I don't cancel, I will receive 6 brand-new novels every month and be billed just $4.49 per book in the U.S. or $4.99 per book in Canada. That's a saving of at least 22% off the cover price. It's quite a bargain! Shipping and handling is just 50¢ per book in the U.S. and 75¢ per book in Canada.* I understand that accepting the 2 free books and gifts places me under no obligation to buy anything. I can always return a shipment and cancel at any time. Even if I never buy another book, the two free books and gifts are mine to keep forever.

105/305 IDN FEGR

Name	(PLEASE PRINT)	

Address		Apt. #

City	State/Prov.	Zip/Postal Code

Signature (if under 18, a parent or guardian must sign)

Mail to the **Reader Service:**
IN U.S.A.: P.O. Box 1867, Buffalo, NY 14240-1867
IN CANADA: P.O. Box 609, Fort Erie, Ontario L2A 5X3

Not valid for current subscribers to Love Inspired books.

**Are you a subscriber to Love Inspired books
and want to receive the larger-print edition?
Call 1-800-873-8635 or visit www.ReaderService.com.**

* Terms and prices subject to change without notice. Prices do not include applicable taxes. Sales tax applicable in N.Y. Canadian residents will be charged applicable taxes. Offer not valid in Quebec. This offer is limited to one order per household. All orders subject to credit approval. Credit or debit balances in a customer's account(s) may be offset by any other outstanding balance owed by or to the customer. Please allow 4 to 6 weeks for delivery. Offer available while quantities last.

Your Privacy—The Reader Service is committed to protecting your privacy. Our Privacy Policy is available online at www.ReaderService.com or upon request from the Reader Service.

We make a portion of our mailing list available to reputable third parties that offer products we believe may interest you. If you prefer that we not exchange your name with third parties, or if you wish to clarify or modify your communication preferences, please visit us at www.ReaderService.com/consumerschoice or write to us at Reader Service Preference Service, P.O. Box 9062, Buffalo, NY 14269. Include your complete name and address.

LIREG11B

Love Inspired
SUSPENSE
RIVETING INSPIRATIONAL ROMANCE

FITZGERALD BAY

Law-enforcement siblings fight for justice and family.

Follow the men and women of Fitzgerald Bay as they unravel the mystery of their small town and find love in the process, with:

THE LAWMAN'S LEGACY by Shirlee McCoy
January 2012

THE ROOKIE'S ASSIGNMENT by Valerie Hansen
February 2012

THE DETECTIVE'S SECRET DAUGHTER
by Rachelle McCalla
March 2012

THE WIDOW'S PROTECTOR by Stephanie Newton
April 2012

THE BLACK SHEEP'S REDEMPTION by Lynette Eason
May 2012

THE DEPUTY'S DUTY by Terri Reed
June 2012

*Available wherever
books are sold.*

www.LoveInspiredBooks.com

LISCONT12